*A
Harlequin
Romance*

OTHER
Harlequin Romances
by KATRINA BRITT

Many of these titles are available at your local bookseller,
or through the Harlequin Reader Service.

For a free catalogue listing all available Harlequin Romances,
send your name and address to:

HARLEQUIN READER SERVICE,
M.P.O. Box 707, Niagara Falls, N.Y. 14302
Canadian address: Stratford, Ontario, Canada.

or use order coupon at back of book.

THE
GUARDED GATES

by

KATRINA BRITT

HARLEQUIN BOOKS   TORONTO
WINNIPEG

Original hard cover edition published in 1973
by Mills & Boon Limited.

© Katrina Britt 1973

SBN 373-01760-X

Harlequin edition published February 1974

Printed in Canada

When Eve passed out of Eden
    Beside its guarded gates
She saw a flower blooming
    Afar from all its mates,
And tearfully she raised it
    And tenderly she bore
    Away from that loved garden
Where she would walk no more.

But grew the flower and flourished
    And lifted up its face
Bright with the Eden beauty,
    Fair with the Eden grace.
Dear blossom of remembrance,
    Blue as its native skies,
    "Forget-me-not", still breathing
    For that lost paradise.

ANNIE JOHNSON FLINT

CHAPTER I

"Why, of course I'll do it," Dionis said rather forcibly, adding a little ruefully, "I wish you hadn't sprung it upon me so precipitately, though."

"You have a week in which to adjust yourself to a change of plan," replied her sister coolly, taking a cigarette from a gold case by her plate at the table. With slow deliberate movements, she flicked a matching lighter taken from her handbag and blew out a line of smoke. "Fortunately, you already have your passport to go to Spain. I know you're keen to see that furnishing exhibition in Madrid. You can still do so – the villa isn't far from Barcelona. I have a picture of it somewhere." She rummaged in her handbag to bring forth a picture postcard which she handed across the table. "Here it is – the Villa Acacia."

"What a perfect pet of a villa!" Dionis exclaimed. The golden glints in her long hazel eyes toning with the lights in her chestnut hair became more pronounced as she stared entranced. "So deliciously Spanish, with the ornamental balconies and all that gorgeous bougainvillea. If the grounds are anything to go by the interior must be lovely too." Steadily, she looked across the table into her sister's cool blue eyes. "You did say Antonio rents it from a distant relative?"

"I did." Angela met the sober gaze with an entirely unconscious expression. "The villa is already furnished. Period stuff," contemptuously. "I want it modernized. All this elegant antique furniture is nice to look at, but not to live with. Not for me, anyway. I like all the modern conveniences."

Dionis looked thoughtfully at her sister's beautifully smooth round face. The dark blue eyes and really flaxen hair were all the more attractive on account of the model figure they were attached to. Her body, long-legged and

7

supple, had rounded curves which she knew how to show to their best advantage. The model suit she wore accentuated every curve seductively to the approaching waiter who was now bringing their coffee after an excellent meal in a new restaurant recently opened in the West End of London. His gaze barely lingered on the hard blue eyes, finding them rather jaded by experience in comparison to the natural freshness of her companion. In his opinion the long hazel eyes of Dionis were definitely more eloquent, more alluring. Her eyelashes, darker than her hair, curled upwards towards neat brows in a small piquant face made for laughter. She thanked him for the coffee with a smile which he returned.

A fascinating creature, he thought, with the most alluring smile he had seen for a long time and a mouth which no man could look upon without wanting to kiss. Definitely the disturbing type, with that fragile, small-boned look making him instantly aware of his own masculinity. Sadly, he walked away, wishing he was twenty years younger.

Unaware of his interest, Dionis stirred her coffee thoughtfully as she spoke.

"This furniture in the Villa Acacia, does it belong to Antonio or the landlord. Most people are rather touchy about there belongings and I dare say the Spanish are no different in that respect from anyone else. It will be moved?"

Angela's laugh grated. "My dear Di, you're far too sentimental." Dionis's concern for the feelings of other people, including those she had never met, amused Angela. "The furniture belongs to the owner, Don Juan Vicente de Velez y Stebelo. Tony is having it stored in the attic," she said flippantly. "Personally, I couldn't care less what's done with it as long as the villa is modernized."

Dionis drank part of her coffee, appalled as usual by Angela's hard streak where getting her own way was concerned. With mixed feelings, she watched the beautifully manicured pink-tipped fingers tap a tube of ash from her cigarette into the ash tray provided before Angela picked up her coffee to the jangle of a lucky charm bracelet on her wrist. As she did so the stream of sunlight blazed on the sapphire engagement ring on her finger. It reminded Dionis that Angela had been engaged four times in as many years since she was twenty-one. Now, at twenty-five, and obviously willing to settle down, providing it was worth her while, she was marrying a Spaniard she had met six months ago while on holiday in Spain.

Angela, a fashion buyer for an exclusive West End salon, travelled extensively in her job. Dionis often found herself wishing, without rancour, that she had some of her sister's poise and self-confidence. But not at the moment. The callous disregard Angela was showing for other people's belongings filled her sister with a primitive and passionate desire to shake some feeling into her.

"Wouldn't it be more satisfactory to have the approval of all concerned? I mean, I've no desire to be a party to upsetting anyone. This relative of Tony's, for instance. Will he mind his furniture being stored?"

Her voice was even enough as she spoke, but Dionis tried in vain to prevent the warm flush rising beneath her clear skin, a fact her sister was quick to notice. Angela controlled herself with an effort. It was really infuriating the way Dionis reminded her that she had a conscience. It was a sensation she particularly disliked, and she hastily tried to be perfectly charming in order to disarm her completely.

"You're worrying unnecessarily, my pet," she said soothingly. "Everything has been taken care of — Tony saw to that before he left for Bermuda. As you know, I'm flying there tonight to join him. So you see you'll have a free hand with no interference from anyone. You can take your time going over the villa and taking down the essentials. Everything you require will be shipped from London in a private container." She drew on her cigarette confidently. "As for the distant relative who owns the villa, he has so much property, one villa more or less isn't going to worry him. He leads a busy life, dividing his time between his residence at Cadiz and another at Castellon. He also has a villa not far from the Villa Acacia, but he rarely uses it. So you won't be bothered with him."

Dionis sighed. It sounded so simple, too simple. "I wish you weren't going away so soon. We really ought to discuss it more fully. It's not as though Bermuda was near enough for us to get in touch quickly in case of emergency," she said, wishing she felt more enthusiastic about it. Vaguely apprehensive, she could not prevent an odd sensation of foreboding rippling along her nerves despite her sister's cool reassurance. If Angela's fiancé had money why did he not build a villa to suit their requirements? Could it be that the distant relative from whom he rented the villa objected to anything modern clashing with the Spanish achitecture of the surrounding countryside?

Angela was saying, "I'm leaving everything to you. You have excellent taste. Who knows? Modernizing the villa might well make you famous in that particular part of Spain. Quite a number of English people are settling there for the sun. When we're married, Tony and I will entertain a great deal. Consequently, the villa will be seen frequently by our guests and you could have orders galore."

The dark blue eyes were suddenly calculating, leaving Dionis in no way deceived by her sister's smooth tongue. She knew Angela was not offering her the job to help to further her career. As usual, she was doing it for her own ends. Angela had a knack of making every advantage to herself appear as a gift from the gods to anyone whose help she enlisted in that direction.

With doubts strangely tangible, Dionis said levelly, "You do intend to marry Tony?"

"Of course I do." Angela blew a practised line of smoke into the air. "Actually, Tony wanted us to get married and go to Bermuda, combining a honeymoon with a business trip. However, I told him that was definitely off. When I marry I want a grand affair with all the trimmings and a honeymoon completely divorced from business of any kind." She admired the sapphire ring on her left hand with some satisfaction. "Why do you ask?"

"Because it would be tragic if you had the Villa Acacia furnished to your own requirements and then broke off the engagement. After all, the villa isn't in London, it's in Spain. If you did decide not to marry Tony he could end by marrying a Spanish girl who would possibly prefer the villa in its original state. Have you thought of that?"

Angela flashed the ring impatiently. "I wear his ring."

"Which I seem to recall is the fifth engagement ring you've worn to date," Dionis commented dryly. "You were equally enthusiastic over your other engagements. Remember Ralph Waldron? You were all set for marriage and a long honeymoon on his yacht when his business wobbled. Then there was Charles Frayne who owned the chain stores. He was too bossy. Clifford Brennan was exciting until . . ."

Angela cut in frigidly. "Please, spare me the post-mortem! At least I didn't marry the first man who asked me. I am endeavouring to get the best out of life."

Dionis shook her head. Her look was tender and sweet. "Angela darling, the only way I know of to get the best out of life is by giving of your best. Please give me your promise to marry the man."

"Don't you preach to me!" Angela was furious. Dionis was relieved that she kept her voice down low enough to blend in with the buzz of conversation going on around them at the other tables. "Look, it would be only too easy for me to put someone else on the job."

"Good luck to them." Dionis answered, in no way perturbed. She was too familiar with her sister's outbursts to be intimidated by them.

The rasping breath coming from Angela's lips was like an engine blowing off steam. She followed it by a deadly calm. Apparently it was essential for her not to alter her plans, for she smiled, a sharp-edged smile suggesting claws well hidden. Thoughtfully she tapped the tube of ash from her cigarette into a pottery ash tray provided. Her voice was low, cajolingly so.

"Don't let's quarrel. You know I would rather you did the job, Di. Besides, this engagement is different from the others. There's something about Spaniards that I find strangely exciting. They're so fervently masculine and courteous. There's an underlying passion in them, making you constantly aware of being a woman."

Dionis said firmly, "That's exactly what's worrying me. Your Spaniard isn't likely to take the brush-off calmly – at least not as calmly as the average Englishman. Besides, I'd hate to see the man left with a constant reminder of you in the modernized Villa Acacia. I know you regard my consideration for other people's feelings as sentimental, but it's the way I am."

Angela stubbed out her cigarette with unnecessary force and finished her coffee. "I'm well aware of that," she said, putting down her cup sharply. "However, you just have to take my word for it." She glanced impatiently at her watch, and picked up her handbag and gloves. "I have an appointment for a facial and hair-do at two with André."

Dionis held out the picture postcard. "Your picture," she said.

Already there was a far-away look in Angela's eyes as though she was well ahead with future plans. "Keep it. Remember, everything is taken care of. You'll hear from Tony in due course. And stop worrying." Slowly she rose to her feet to smile down at her sister's anxious gaze. "I know you won't let me down. Take care of yourself."

"You too."

Dionis swallowed a rough obstruction in her throat and looked dazedly at a small packet Angela had pushed across the table towards her. Then she was watching her sister walk gracefully across the dining-room to the pay desk, the cynosure of male eyes. Dionis returned her wave as she left and opened the small packet to see a bottle of exclusive French perfume. How typical of Angela, she thought despairingly, so ruthless and so generous.

Was it only that morning that Angela had arrived jubilantly from a trip to Paris, her last trip for her firm before checking out as Tony's fiancée? Putting the perfume in her handbag, she lingered over the last of her coffee, endeavouring to keep pace with the events almost sweeping her off her feet. The assignment to modernize the Villa Acacia had come out of the blue. While she had recognised it as a heaven-sent opportunity to prove her ability in foreign fields, Dionis wished she could feel more enthusiastic about it. Glancing around the spacious dining-room, she appraised the modern décor of bold colours, the clever murals and cunningly placed lights. What an exciting world interior decorating opened up! She knew she was a natural at it. The endless thrill of matching exclusive designs and shades, creating beauty from drabness and squalor and seeing it all come to life gave one a deep satisfying feeling of achievement. Yet while she loved the unlimited scope of colour and the bold designs of modern trends, she retained a deep respect for elegant antique furniture and works of art.

Putting down her cup, Dionis looked again at the picture of the Villa Acacia, exuding a whiff of Angela's favourite perfume. Did Angela's fiancé share her preference for a modern villa? Dionis knew none of its history, tragic or gay. She attributed it with all the sadness of far-off things, hallowed by the gentle fingers of time. The garden was beautiful and spelled romance to her quick imaginative brain. She hoped the furniture had been stored away when she arrived. She was not at all enthusiastic about stripping the place of all its character to fill it with alien furnishings. Maybe she was too sensitive about it. Angela could be right – life was much simpler when viewed from a practical angle. Placing the postcard of the villa in her handbag, she drew out her purse, intent upon leaving a generous tip. It was not as much as she had intended, but she gave all the coins she had in her purse, searching for a five-pound note as she did so. It was not there, although she had it the previous evening. Then she recalled Angela borrowing it from her that very morning until she went to the bank. Paying for the lunch had been Angela's way of returning it. Oh, to be like Angela!

The last week Dionis was at home simply flew. She shopped for gay sandals, beach wear and day and evening dresses, drawing recklessly on her savings. Slacks and a pretty top were her usual working attire. However, she was going to a foreign country not so advanced as gay, go-ahead London. Besides, the Villa Acacia might be in a place where conventions were a religion, so she would go prepared for any eventuality. Looking back, she could still not quite take it in that she was working for herself. The decision had followed several successful jobs she had undertaken, two of which had been furnishing and decorating a children's home and a home for the elderly.

Both assignments had been given to her by her employer with absolute confidence in her ability to carry them out. Cesare Delusi, a versatile Italian, was a genius in his job as an interior decorator of modernistic design. Well past the early stage of delicate experimenting, he now juggled confidently with brilliant variations and themes, each one sculptured, each dynamically successful. It was he who had encouraged her to branch out on her own, giving her his blessing plus an offer to help her out of any difficulty. Delusi was a household name, and anyone who had been employed by him was invariably assured of a successful future. For her first lone assignment, Dionis had decorated a luxury penthouse for a wealthy pop singer, who had been delighted with the result. When orders began to pour in, Dionis had completed those demanding her immediate attention. The others she had left in abeyance while she took a short holiday abroad, taking in the Modern Furnishing Exhibition in Madrid. Decorating the Villa Acacia would change her little jaunt into a kind of busman's holiday, and she set off full of youthful enthusiasm.

The journey to Spain proved to be uneventful. Arriving in Barcelona, Dionis saw Gaudi's famous church, a bull-ring of Moorish design, and was driven across an impressive modern bridge with four stone eagles on stone pillars set high above it. Soon the industrial suburbs were left behind for flat uninteresting country. Her travelling companions were a mixed bag of tourists and housewives who were returning to outlying farms after shopping. The older women were proud and dignified in their black clothes. The younger ones were more talkative and decidedly pretty. Everyone was happy and no one except Dionis appeared to be in the least put out at the erratic way in which the bus was being driven. Dionis sat gripping her seat as they skidded around blind corners at a terrifying speed, missing pannier-laden donkeys by a hair's breadth. Dionis was surprised on looking back to see the gentle creatures still on their feet plodding on.

Fields scarlet with poppies and green with vines flashed by with the bus gradually slackening speed. They were now passing scattered farms, and presently the driver pulled up with a shrieking of brakes to let down passengers. Then they were off again at the same terrifying speed along white roads where the early evening sun shed a rosy glow over vineyards, irrigated fields and distant hills. Wearily, now Dionis began to look for landmarks. According to the instructions sent to her in a letter from Angela's fiancé, she should now be nearing the inn where he had booked her in for the length of her stay in Spain. Yes – still clutching the back of the seat in front, she could see the hill of three windmills, a definite landmark since she believed the inn was a little further on.

"The *señorita* from Inglaterra!"

The driver's raucous voice startled her as much as the violent jerk of the bus as he hastily jammed on the brakes. Fortunately for Dionis, she was still hanging on to the seat or she would certainly have been shot down the gangway and through the windscreen. Shakenly, she rose to her feet and reached for her small case from the bus rack. The rest of her luggage was in the boot of the bus. With surprising agility for his great bulk, the driver was out of his seat and heaving her cases from the boot. To her surprise he carried them across the white dusty road into the courtyard of the inn, where she rewarded him with a generous amount of pesetas.

The soft glow of evening filtered through the lemon trees

enclosing the courtyard. Dionis looked upon small tables and chairs set out in shade before looking towards the patio. Through the open door of the inn shining brass and cool white walls looked cool and inviting after the heat of the bus. The air was filled with the perfume of flowers, scarlet bougainvillea blooming against outside walls, climbing roses, jasmine and orange blossom abounded. She breathed it in deeply, loving warmth, the colour.

"Señorita Ward?"

The alien tones softly spoken in English roused her and she turned to see a plump little woman shapely in her black dress whose full dark eyes regarded her kindly.

"*Si*. Señora Lopez?" Dionis proceeded to air a little of her elementary knowledge of Spanish.

The *señora* smiled, inclining her head. "*Si, señorita*. You are expected. Please to come this way."

Señora Lopez led the way indoors to a small reception desk where Dionis signed the visitors' book and filled in a registration card. On their way upstairs the *señora* informed Dionis that she was the only guest. Alterations were being carried out at the back of the inn and no more visitors were being accepted until the work was finished. Don Antonio had booked the *señorita*'s rooms some time ago and Señora Lopez understood that Dionis would be out all day except for meals. Lunch would be at two-thirty, tea at six with dinner at ten.

Dionis wondered if the *señora* knew the nature of her visit and decided it was not important. The conversation had taken them to a bedroom where a four-poster bed with a colourful woven bedspread gave a gay air to sombre furniture. Hot and sticky and a trifle weary, Dionis eased off her small white hat, pushed pearl-tipped fingers through the heavy waves of hair and looked at windows shuttered against the heat.

"The Villa Acacia, is it far away?" she asked, perhaps foolishly, for Tony would naturally book her into the nearest inn.

"No, Miss Ward. The Quinta Acacia is but a little way

up the road from here." Señora Lopez walked gracefully to the window facing them and opened the shutters. "See, there it is through the trees."

Dionis saw a pretty red roof in a panoramic view of vast blue sky etched by trees and bounded by distant hills. Maybe it was because she had already seen a picture of the villa that the scene confronting her appeared more familiar than strange. Indeed it seemed that the hot sun, the perfumed air and clearly defined beauty of the landscape were all combined in a welcome so warm that she had the feeling of belonging. Señora Lopez had put her immediately at her ease and Dionis thanked her warmly as she withdrew. With the best part of two hours before dinner was served at ten, she made her way to the bathroom where she discovered a newly installed shower by the rather antiquated bath.

Under the shower she washed away the stickiness of travel, used the soft fluffy towels and creamed the dryness from her skin brought on by the heat and dust. The cleanliness and homely atmosphere banished her weariness and she hummed softly when she returned to her room to find her cases had been brought up. The second window of her room overlooked the courtyard where a sudden cackle made her open the shutters to look down. A goose was waddling over the cobblestones of the courtyard below. So that was where the inn got its name – El Ganso. The Goose. It seemed that Spain, like Rome, regarded geese as watchdogs.

Dionis emptied her cases, filling cupboards and drawers smelling sweetly of pot-pourri, debating as she did so whether a life free from ties was not the best kind after all. Her thoughts dwelt on her father, visualizing a laughing, daring man who as a successful racing motorist had travelled the most dangerous circuits in the world only to meet his death on a quiet English country road one fateful Sunday afternoon. Her mother had met him at the airport after a successful Grand Prix and they had been driving back to their home in Surbiton when a stolen car driven by two youths had crashed into them head-on. Death had been instantaneous for them both.

Dionis had been eight and Angela eleven at the time. They had been brought up by their paternal grandparents, who had seen both girls launched in their respective careers before emigrating to Canada to join their other son. Dionis loved her grandparents dearly, and had clung to her grandfather on the quay where she and Angela had gone to see them off.

Her grandfather had said, "I'm not so upset at leaving Angela as you, my poppet." His deep-set eyes beneath shaggy brows had been directed towards her sister who, perfectly composed, was talking to her grandmother. "Granted, she's only three years older than you, but she's always been able to look after number one. Whereas she allows her head to rule her heart, you're inclined to do the opposite. However," he had counselled wisely, "keep your illusions, providing you keep your rose-coloured spectacles well polished in order to be able to see beyond them if the occasion arises."

Had she rose-coloured spectacles? Dionis wondered. She only knew that the tender care of grandparents had resulted in her growing up in a happy uncomplicated way. And so far Spain had lived up to her expectations – the warmth, the courteousness, were there. When she had put away her empty cases Dionis saw there was time for a quick visit to the Villa Acacia. Eager to see it at close quarters, she draped a white woolly jacket over her blue suit and went quietly downstairs. An appetizing aroma of food came from the kitchen and she could hear the sounds of activity. Should she ask particulars about the villa, whether she would need a key or if there were caretakers there? Reluctant to trespass on the *señora*'s domain, especially as she was busy preparing dinner. Dionis decided to stroll along to see what the situation was. Silently she passed through the courtyard empty except for a white cat who came to rub against her leg purring fondly.

"Aren't you lovely?" she said, bending to stroke the soft thick fur before going on her way. Strolling along the white dusty road in the warm summer evening, she was instantly aware of the brilliantly clear air and the intoxicating vividness of her surroundings. There was not the fresh green of her beloved England but the clarity of light, light so powerful that everything, trees, hills and villas, was outlined in a vividness stirring to the senses. It was like some powerful drug giving her a palpably keen observation of everything around her. The vast area of sky burnt to gold by the sun, the red-gold distances where the faint tinkle of goat bells drew her gaze to a goatherd sharply outlined in the oblique light, filled her with wonder. He stood with his cloak thrown carelessly over one shoulder giving a dramatic air to a scene which could have belonged to an old Spanish painting. Gradually Dionis felt the power and languor wrapping her pleasantly in a cocoon of warmth which numbed her senses.

Then she saw the Villa Acacia, looking just like the photograph except that now it bore a neglected air. It was a long white building with a belfry, a pillared patio and a porch topped by a trellis of vines casting lacy shadows in the late evening sun. A profusion of scarlet flowers spilled from behind iron balconies set against windows scenting the air with their fragrance. The silence was tangible as she walked through the garden overgrown with weeds and creepers to the ornate bell-pull at the side of the front door. There was no reply to the hollow sound reverberating through the villa and she stepped back to look up at closed shutters. Then making her way to the back of the house she strolled, paused and wandered in a trance staring at tangled thorns, creepers and dead branches. At length she sat down on a marble seat half hidden by creepers and trailing roses cascading down from the high stone wall behind her and endeavoured to take stock.

Looking around, Dionis could see that in this rich sun-soaked land everything grew with mercurial swiftness. Obviously the villa had not been empty long. That being so, the task of putting the garden to rights was not too formidable. A good man could do it in a couple of weeks. She would ask Señora Lopez if she knew of such a man. Apart from making the place look more inviting it was essential to have it done as soon as possible before it grew worse.

The villa was enchanting and she could visualize the grounds when they were immaculate once more, forming a perfect frame for the modern interior. Closing her eyes, Dionis felt the charm of the place washing over her in fragrant waves. What utter bliss it would be to spend a summer here ! She could fit so easily into this life in the sun with its brilliant contrasts of colour, its sense of timelessness in a majesty of landscape which filled her with awe. The casual stroll back to the inn was extremely pleasant and she found herself looking forward to her late meal.

The courtyard of the inn looked cool and inviting with the gay little tables spotlighted by beams from an orange sun filtering through the foliage of the lemon trees overhead. An olive-skinned girl in a black dress and swinging gypsy earrings hummed softly to herself as she set one of the tables. She was vital and alive, lifting dark eyes remarkably like those of the *señora* when Dionis appeared.

"Buenos noches, señorita," she said, resorting to English with a flashing smile. "I am Tercia, the daughter of Señora Lopez. I am to tell you that everything is ready when you are."

Dionis smiled in return, warming to her fresh young look. *"Gracias,* Tercia. I shall be down immediately."

When she returned, Tercia was touching the pretty flower arrangement in the centre of the table. She straightened on seeing Dionis and drew out her chair with an inviting gesture. Seconds later she whisked away in a manner so sparkling, so effervescent, as to leave Dionis feeling nondescript and negligible. She felt like some pale ghost escaped from another planet, tempted by the loveliness of this Eden set in a foreign country. This young sultry creature, although younger than her own twenty-two years, bubbled with life. Belonging to a race whose blood ran more swiftly through their veins, she was capable of intense emotion, of violent likes and dislikes. It stemmed from the hot sun, the vastness of the skies, and was reflected in smouldering dark eyes through which powerful unspoken communications were transmitted at a glance. Dionis, taking stock of her own placid existence, realized that while she had not scaled any great heights, she had not reached any great depths either. Her sense of isolation was muted by a drowsy warmth of goodwill and a tranquillity she had not known for a long time.

The meal was simple by Spanish standards, cooked perfectly over a charcoal fire which Tercia assured her was responsible for its excellent flavour. Dionis enjoyed the iced soup, a stimulating aperitif for the omelette and chicken cooked with tarragon which followed. She sensed Tercia's friendly curiosity as she brought each course; the girl probably found her as alien as she found herself. She was nearing the end of her meal when she saw Tercia leaving the courtyard preceded by the short stocky figure of a man.

"Tercia has gone with her father to the house of her *novio*." Señora Lopez was there with freshly brewed coffee. "She is engaged. In two or three years perhaps she will marry. Tercia is now but seventeen."

"So long?" Dionis asked wonderingly, watching the graceful movements of the *señora's* hands pouring out the coffee.

"*Sí.* Tercia and her *novio* have known each other's ways less than six months. Before that they communicated through Miguel's brother. It is the custom," said the *señora* tranquilly.

"Their marriage was arranged, of course."

Señora Lopez smiled. "Both families hoped for the match. Miguel fell in love with Tercia when she was fifteen. He was nineteen. Tercia adores him. But it is well that they should reach a more discerning age before they marry."

The *señora* gathered the used dishes together and departed, leaving Dionis to enjoy her coffee. With her eyes fixed dreamily upon the shadows through which Tercia and her father had disappeared, Dionis saw the girl's future as being poles apart from that of an English girl. Not for Tercia the modern conveniences which the average English-woman claimed as her right. A charcoal fire and braziers to keep out the winter's bite would be Tercia's only luxuries.

The light was fading now filling the courtyard with shadows. The cloistered courtyard with its mixed fragrance of charcoal and lavender and the excellent meal were having their effect. Dionis felt drowsy, but it was a drowsiness underlaid with a strange restlessness. The night was far too beautiful for her to leave it and go to bed. She was contemplating taking a walk when a thought inhibited her. In Spain young women did not go out alone at night. It simply was not done, not even by Englishwomen, unless they wished to make themselves conspicuous. She had already defied the conventions by going alone to the Villa Acacia. It seemed she had no choice. Rising reluctantly, Dionis was about to walk to her room when the glow of a brazier in the small covered patio to the right of the porch caught her eye. Señora Lopez stood on a stool lighting the brass hanging lamp attached to the patio ceiling.

"*Gracias* for a wonderful meal, Señora Lopez. I enjoyed it very much," Dionis assured her sincerely.

The *señora* stepped from the stool and set it in a corner. "I am happy that you are satisfied, Miss Ward. Pray do not go to your room. Come, sit for a while on the patio. The night is young and we in Spain do not retire early. For most of us the day is just beginning."

She gestured to a cushioned seat running the length of the pillared patio by the wall. A glowing brazier filled the air warmly, keeping at bay the slow drop in temperature that the night invariably brings. They sat side by side facing the glow. Beneath the soft light of the hanging lamp the *señora's* hair shone like the blue-black plumage of a bird. For all her plumpness she was decorous, with her tiny hands and feet, fine ankles and expressive eyes. It occurred to Dionis how much more feminine a woman appeared when she was modest and well versed in the arts of being a

22

woman. Englishwomen had lost some of the art of sitting decorously since they chose to wear trousers.

The *señora*'s dark eyes suddenly met her own. "I have the key to the Villa Acacia, Miss Ward. You will be going there tomorrow?"

"Yes." Dionis did not enlighten her about her recent visit. She decided not to mention it until she knew how much the *señora* knew of her reason for being there. At an inn there was always a considerable amount of gossip going on. Fortunately, she was the only guest at the moment, which was just as well.

"Did Don Antonio have a housekeeper?" she asked casually.

"*Si.* A woman from the village came each day to cook and clean. Since Don Antonio left, Paco the gardener has been in charge. Unfortunately, he strained his knee and has been away. He lives with his sister in the village." She shrugged philosophically. "Do not expect to see him at work when you arrive there tomorrow. He has promised to return to work this week. It is possible for him to put in an appearance before lunch. After lunch is the siesta, so he might return after four in the afternoon. Then, Miss Ward, Paco will work like two horses until quite late." She lifted her head and Dionis, following her gaze, saw a short broad-set elderly man entering the courtyard. "*Buenos noches*, Don Fernando," she exclaimed welcoming the newcomer with a smile. "Miss Ward, may I present Don Fernando de Peralto, a very old friend and the plague of my life."

"*Buenos noches.*" He bowed courteously over Dionis's hand. His clothes were of an expensive cut although worn to his figure, his face had the sallowness of middle age, but his dark eyes were young and glowing. It was left to the small beard, precision-cut, to give his face the strength of character which Dionis found so arresting.

He had been followed into the courtyard by several men who made their way inside the inn to take wine. Dionis was about to make her own excuses and go to her room when the *señora* went to serve the men. After all, Don Fernando was a perfect stranger and she might find it difficult to make conversation with him. Yet she hesitated, feeling his courteousness and air of understanding like a gentle restraining hand upon her shoulder bidding her to stay. He had taken the stool the *señora* had used when she lit the lamp and now she was back carrying a tray containing two glasses of wine and a box of cigars. Don Fernando leaned forward to help himself to a cigar and the *señora* snicked a lighter.

"I don't know what you would do without your glass of wine and cigar, Don Fernando," she said teasingly, placing a glass of wine on a low table near him and offering Dionis the other. "This is on the house. I think you will like it — it is a local brew, but a good one. Now, if you will excuse me I will return to attend to my customers."

Dionis graciously accepted the wine, although she wondered if she had room for it after the very satisfying dinner. Feeling Don Fernando's eyes upon her, she drank a little.

"Good?" he asked in English.

"Very," she replied, as indeed it was. "Do you speak English, *señor*?"

"*Si*. I have conversed with many of your countrymen over the years on this very spot and have enjoyed every moment of it."

Dionis warmed to his air of gentleness accoladed by a pleasing dignity suggesting great wisdom and tolerance. His whole bearing showed him to be a man of breeding and intelligence. He smoked his cigar while Dionis sat content to savour the beauty of the evening in the company of a man she felt instinctively that she could trust. She fell to thinking of her reason for being there and wished she could have been there earlier in order to see her sister and Antonio together. Witnessing Angela's reaction to her fiancé might have convinced her of her sister's sincerity. Past experience had made Dionis wary where Angela's love life was concerned. To most women, a man, a home and children were the ultimate aims in life. While her sister

24

might not be capable of a deep and abiding love for any one man, Dionis doubted whether she would be content with the affection of a husband and family. There would have to be the added excitements of all that wealth could bring. How could Antonio be wealthy when he rented a villa from a distant relative? The fact that Angela had fallen in love with the country could strengthen her resolve to marry her Tony and settle down at the villa. Dionis fervently hoped so.

"Did you have a good journey?" Don Fernando asked. "You will soon settle and become one of us."

Dionis smiled and nodded. The wine had imparted an inner glow. If the lovely evenings were to be the end of each working day then she was certainly looking forward to them. The warmth of her welcome had been most reassuring, Don Fernando's company enchanting. He was studying her now with a keen shrewd gaze.

"Forgive me, Miss Ward, for using the old approach of suggesting that you and I could have met before. Apart from the fact of your name being familiar the shape of your face, the faint charming slant to those lovely long eyes and a certain cadence in your voice all strike a chord in my memory."

A small pleat deepened between her neat eyebrows. She smiled comprehendingly.

"My sister Angela was here a short while ago. It is possible that you met her. But she is nothing like me. She is blonde and beautiful."

"And are you not beautiful, Miss Ward? Beauty is in the eye of the beholder." His smile was a wise one. "I remember your sister — the *novia* of Don Antonio." He stroked his small beard reflectively. "*Si*, you both have that family likeness. You also bear the same name of a very dear friend of mine who passed away some years ago in tragic circumstances."

"Ward is a fairly common name in England, *señor*," Dionis assured him.

There was sadness in the dark eyes and a far-away look.

"My friend was English also. He had two small daughters and a wife whom he adored. It is all of fourteen years since he died. Yet I can see him as though it was only yesterday sitting in the very place you now occupy." He shook his head sadly. "He was so much in love with life and eager for the thrills it offered. So sad that after touring all the most dangerous racing circuits in the world he should meet his end on one of your quiet country roads."

Dionis was experiencing a tide of emotion coupled with a strange excitement.

"Fourteen years ago, señor, I was eight years old. My father died that year in similar circumstances. He was also a well-known racing driver. Your friend's name? Was it . . ." But Dionis was unable to say more. Her lips were too unsteady to form the words.

"His name was Alexander John Ward."

"He was my father, señor."

"But this is wonderful, Miss Ward! It is indeed a small world. I am greatly honoured to make your acquaintance. I had a younger brother also a racing driver. Alas, he was killed on the track. Your father stopped his own car during that fateful race in order to try to pull my young brother clear of the blazing car. But it was too late."

"I'm sorry, señor."

Don Fernando nodded his head. His eyes were shadowed with unhappy memories.

"Señor Ward tried to take his place by calling to see us as often as he could. He helped us a great deal in the first difficult months of bereavement. Your father was a remarkable person."

"I was so young when he died. My memories of him are neither very clear nor are they many. Please tell me how you met him and all about him," Dionis implored.

"What can I say except that he was one of those clean-limbed young Englishmen it has always been a pleasure to meet. You are very much like him."

Dionis's eyes were wide with surprise. "Really? My father was fair-haired and blue-eyed, more like Angela."

"In colouring, perhaps, but his true character and personality live again in you, *niña*. You have inherited all that made him great – his ideals, integrity and tolerance and his zest for life. All are mirrored in those long dark eyes of yours which are as eloquent as once his were."

Dionis flushed with pleasure. "How sweet of you to say that, because now I feel as if he had never left me." She smiled demurely. "I don't think I'm as courageous as he was, but it's nice of you to say so."

"You are brave enough to strive to do the right thing, and you like people." His glance flickered over her, kindly and analytical. Dionis looked startled.

"But how can you tell? We've only just met," she cried.

"Intuition and the experience of an old man."

"I can't believe it!" she breathed with stars in her eyes. "To think that my father actually sat here and talked to you as I am now. You have no idea what it means to me to know that." She laughed, an enchanting laugh of pure happiness. "I can never feel strange here again after what you have told me."

Don Fernando, cigar in hand, studied the ash as he spoke. "Your first impressions of us will account for everything appearing alien to you. Yet, like you, we belong to an ancient race of people who have clung to our ideals. We still cling to the old traditions, more violently perhaps because we live nearer to the soil. But our fundamental desires remain the same."

They talked for a long time, with Don Fernando answering her eager questions with courtesy and charm. Dionis felt she would always remember her first evening in Spain with the patio bathed in a golden glow from the gilt hanging lamp and the softly burning brazier. Don Fernando's cigar mingled with the nocturnal scents of exotic blooms set against white walls and rich dark shadows. She thought of her father with a little thrill of pride. Because of him the inn had become an enchanted place.

CHAPTER II

DIONIS awoke to the cackle of geese and the tinkle of goat bells. For bewildered sleepy moments her eyes roved around the strange room. The cool beauty of tiled floors covered by delicately coloured rugs which toned with the gay counterpanes, old Spanish furniture against white walls, a neat classic study coming to life beneath the gentle fingers of sun pushing through the shutters. Instinctively, her eyes were drawn to the dressing table on which lay the keys to the Villa Acacia given to her the previous evening by Señora Lopez. While she was eager to start to work again she was also aware of a strange foreboding.

This strange reluctant feeling at the start of a new assignment was as unfamiliar as it was unsettling. Somehow the thought of her father being held in such high esteem by the local people added to her uneasiness. She wanted nothing to happen to spoil that image. Padding to her window, she opened the shutters to breathe in the perfume of climbing roses. Tercia was crossing the courtyard below carrying a pitcher of milk. Her full-skirted dress swung from swaying hips and the sun glinted on the Spanish gypsy ear-rings. She was singing, but stopped immediately her mother appeared telling her to be quiet. Then the *señora* was stepping back to look up at Dionis's window before following her gay daughter indoors. Dionis waved.

She had showered and put on a wrap when Tercia appeared with her breakfast — fruit juice, fresh rolls, home-made cherry jam and honey. The coffee was delicious. Well fortified inwardly for work on the Villa Acacia, Dionis put on a suit in navy sailcloth trimmed with white, trod into white sandals, armed herself with a pad and pencil and picking up her bag went out to do battle. Downstairs she exchanged greetings with Señora Lopez, who was pleased to hear that she had slept well.

"You will be in to lunch, Miss Ward, at two-thirty?" she queried.

"Si, señora, unless you would prefer me to take a picnic lunch," Dionis replied thoughtfully.

"No, no. You will come back to the inn for lunch, then upstairs to your siesta. You will work much better when your return to the villa later," the señora said firmly.

Dionis capitulated nicely, although, in her opinion, the siesta was a bore, making a big break in her working day and one she had not foreseen. She opened the gate to the Villa Acacia, once more shuttered and secret, and walked through the overgrown garden, taking deep breaths of the perfumed air. The señora had been right about Paco the gardener. He had not arrived. In the silence, Dionis found it easy to regard it all as a dream. Externally, the Villa Acacia was beautiful, a joy to look at. The baroque-panelled front door sheltered by a classical porch was enriched by ornamental brackets. She appreciated the entrance being placed more to one side of the façade instead of dead centre, thus ensuring that there was no through-draught to the back of the villa. When she opened the door, she stood for several moments feeling excited and strangely breathless.

As she had hoped, the furniture had been removed, and the interior was sweet and clean. In the hall the exquisite Moorish tiled floor was dominated by a graceful staircase which curved upwards to the first floor. The motifs in the wrought iron balustrade were charming, so were the arched doorways. The one to the left led to the dining-room, kitchen, larder and back door. To the right were the study, lounge, library, cloakrooms and nursery. Dionis loved the nursery, picturing a dimpled, chuckling baby blowing bubbles to the sun outside on the patio overlooking the kitchen garden. With dreams in her eyes, she gazed at the open fireplace, the lovely ceiling from which polished brass lamps hung gleaming softly in the muted sunlight streaming through the shutters.

It was evident from the immaculate condition of the walls

and ceilings that the whole interior had not long been decorated throughout. The planning of the ground floor had accomplished the intention of smaller villas in the distribution of rooms with their easy access from one to another. The plan was repeated all through the villa, giving a feeling of spaciousness. There were three bedrooms, dressing-rooms and bathrooms. All were high-ceilinged and roomy. Looking up at magnificent alabaster carving and cornices, Dionis pictured a deep contrasting colour against paler walls. The bedroom furniture in built-in units would be ideal, but not against the outer walls where they would be open to damp and condensation when the temperature rose or fell. They could be fixed to the inner walls where they would strengthen the partitions between rooms. The charm of the place filled her with delight as she measured up the rooms and jotted down details in her notebook. She discovered that the master bedroom had a degree of privacy with each room opening out on to the landing instead of leading into each other like the rest. Already she was visualizing a white wool covering on the walls enhanced by rich cream transparent drapes fully gathered and reaching to the floor. The heavy draw curtains would be cream laced with cinnamon with a matching bedspread in a chunkier fabric. Generously built-in furniture would mean that the rest of the room would only need the minimum of furniture. Two petal-shaped chairs in white cane to match the built-in units would be ideal.

It was heartening to have a free hand with no one butting in to stem her flow of ideas. And it was a great help to have the rooms cleared of furniture. Curious as to where it had been stored, Dionis made her way up to the top floors built in the rafters and gingerly opened a door. The furniture was there. Rather guiltily she glimpsed a charming lacquer cabinet, really lovely tapestry-upholstered chairs and several intriguing little footstools before she gently closed the door. She hoped nothing would deteriorate with storage. While the villa appeared to be in excellent condition any defect in the roof could allow rain to come in and ruin the furniture beyond repair. She might be worrying over nothing. Anyway, it was no business of hers, she concluded as she descended the stairs.

It was suffocatingly hot in the midday sun when Dionis went to the porched entrance to hear the scuffed sound of rope-soled espadrilles on the garden path. And suddenly there was Paco. A thick-set figure of medium height wearing neat and patched clothes, he came forward shyly, hat in hand, his small eyes shiny as black olives.

"*Buenos dios, señorita,*" he said, continuing in halting English, "I must apologize for the state of the garden, but I have hurt my knee." He gestured to his left leg where a neat patch on his trousers covered the offending limb. "I have almost recovered. The pain now is only irritating to me because I have never been ill. I am as strong as an ox – anyone in the village will tell you." He straightened proudly and smiled, showing rather yellow strong teeth. His sallow face had a melancholy look, but Dionis took to him on sight. He could be around fifty, but he obviously was rather sweet and naïve as he added shyly, "I am Paco."

"You're not to worry about the garden, Paco. Accidents will happen. You must be sure the knee is quite well before you start to use it," Dionis said with a gentle smile.

"I am sure, *señorita.* Señor Juan Vicente de Velez y Stebelo would be angry to see the garden so. I will start immediately to put it to rights," he said with a quaint dignity.

Suddenly Dionis was looking overhead where a great bird had appeared to hover ominously. In that split second it swooped into the branches of a tree nearby and emerging silently with its prey, it swooped away into the blue distance. So sudden, so unerringly direct was it that Dionis stared in a fascinated horror. She shivered in the heat to meet Paco's sympathetic gaze.

"*Mas vale que Fuerza, señorita,*" he quoted. "Skill is better than strength."

For a long moment they looked at each other with Dionis experiencing an emotion more disturbing than anything

31

she had ever known. Was it the bird of prey showing her the cruelty of nature here as anywhere else? Or was it the mention of Don Juan? So he would be angry over the state of the garden. She only hoped he had given permission for the conversion of the villa, that was all.

Putting the incident behind her rather sadly, she said, "I'm sure it won't take long to put to rights. But whatever you do you must not tire the knee. I want your promise on that, Paco."

"*Gracias, señorita*. You have my word." He had brightened at her obvious concern. "I have relatives, all craftsmen, who would gladly assist the *señorita* in her work in the villa. You have only to say the word."

"*Gracias*, Paco. I shall certainly need them when my materials arrive. I will let you know."

Dionis watched him amble to the garden shed for his tools. He really was a pet, she thought, returning to the villa to make a final check before she left for lunch. Paco had gone when she finally emerged from the villa. The sun blazed down on her uncovered head and she arrived back at the inn hot and thirsty. She ate her lunch at one of the small tables under the lemon trees in the courtyard – gazpacho soup, ice-cold, both an aperitif and a delicious thirst-quencher. Ham, meat, cheese, fruit and crisp rolls with fresh butter followed. There was a rosé wine and mineral water. Dionis chose the latter.

After lunch, she went to her cool shuttered room for the siesta. Lying on her bed, she tried to relax, but her thoughts were too occupied with her job. Her brain was afire with plans inspired by the blue distances, the velvet illusions of light and shade, the shimmering radiance of exotic colours, the sudden richness of black and white. She was impatient to start and found herself hoping that her work would meet with Antonio's approval and Don Juan Stebelo's also. Now why on earth should she think of Don Juan, a man she had never met and was not likely to meet.

A quarter of an hour lying on her back and Dionis had had enough. She had a wash and brush up and was again on her way out. Silence greeted her as she went quietly downstairs. The inn was shuttered and silent. No sound came from the kitchens or any part of the house. The white cat stretched out beneath the lemon trees did not bother to lift its head when she walked across the courtyard. The white dusty road unwound slowly before her in a fragrant aura of lavender and wild thyme, and when the sudden clip-clop of a horse's hooves drew nearer behind her, Dionis drew in at the side of the road.

"*Buenos tardes*, Miss Ward," came the familiar voice, and she stopped as a horse-drawn carriage drew up beside her. Don Fernando's face beneath his straw hat beamed as he offered a hand with Spanish gallantry to help her up beside him. "Are you not enjoying the siesta?" he asked on a surprised note.

"I'm eager to get on with the job," she admitted frankly, sitting beside him all smiles. "Besides, it's cool inside the villa. You do know I'm decorating it in the modern style, *señor*?"

"*Si*. I was at the inn the night Don Antonio came to book rooms for you. So it makes two of us abroad in the sun when we ought to be taking our siesta. I am not doing it by choice. I am on my way to pick up Inez, my wife. She is visiting a sick friend and wanted to be home for the siesta. Unfortunately, the horse cast a shoe and I am well over an hour late at calling for Inez."

"She'll be wondering what's keeping you. Isn't this lovely?" Dionis watched the gay blue and white tassels swinging on the harness as the horse trotted proudly along.

"You do not find it tame after your fast cars?"

"Not at all. It is most relaxing, and quite the perfect way of seeing the countryside." She was smiling at him when a tornado in the shape of a long silver car shot past, leaving them in a cloud of white dust. "My goodness," she gasped, "it seems you have your road-hogs here too, *señor*!"

He shrugged resignedly. "All part of the mechanical age which is creeping into every country these days. Fortunately, we don't see many cars on these byways where donkeys are invariably used."

When he dropped her off at the Villa Acacia, his eyes rested upon her uncovered head. "You did say you were working indoors?"

"I did." She smiled somewhat ruefully. "I know I should be wearing a hat and it's very remiss of me. I forgot sunglasses too."

He shook his head in mild reproof. "That is one thing you will learn while you are here – to take your time. The true Spaniard takes his time and savours life to the full."

"I'll remember that – and please call me Dionis."

"With pleasure, Dionis. I am Fernando to all my friends."

"*Adios*, Don Fernando. *Gracias* for the lift. It was lovely."

Walking through the garden of the villa, Dionis knew Paco would not be back until after the siesta, and not then if his knee troubled him. Siesta could mean any time up to four, which was the hour when the shops opened again. He had cleared away quite a quantity of dead leaves, weeds and branches and piled them into a compost heap in a corner of the garden. She could hardly wait to see it restored to all its former glory. There, for instance, by the solid thick stone wall was a pretty bird table. It was almost entirely hidden with trailing vines which she pulled in an effort to tear them away. They were stubborn and strong, defying all her efforts to dislodge them. Warming to her task, she found secateurs in the garden shed and set to work in earnest. What treasures she uncovered – oleanders, myrtles, nasturtiums and camellias nestling in their beds of cool damp earth beneath the tangles of weeds.

She had cleared the bird table when she saw the garden seat. Intrigued, she started to clear this too, discovering to her delight that it was pure marble exquisitely tiled in garden scenes. The scrolled effect of the arms and the back of the seat formed a perfect frame for the pretty scenes depicted in really lovely pastel colours. It was hard work dislodging all the thick growth choking it. A man would have accomplished it in half the time and the sun was really far too hot for such demanding work, but Dionis kept doggedly on until her back began to ache and her head throb from the heat of the sun.

Her clothes clung moistly to her skin and she was exhausted by the time the seat was finally cleared. She forgot her discomfort as she gazed in admiration at the work of art depicted by the tiles. Then suddenly the seat was blotted out by a red glow beneath her eyelids accompanied by a giddy feeling of nausea. Blinking furiously to dispel it, she turned. The car moved smoothly, making scarcely a sound, and drew up not many yards from where she stood.

Dionis seemed scarcely to breathe. She watched the car arrive and the man who got out of it with the feeling of never having met anyone so repellently remote, so ... so perfectly high-bred and regal. He was of medium height, lean and spare with the suggestion of hidden strength in the wide shoulders. His ears were set closely against a well-shaped head which he carried proudly, almost haughtily. His olive features were lean-cut and handsome. From the high noble forehead, long nose with slightly flaring nostrils down to the mobile mouth and well-defined jaw, he exuded power and authority. He was immaculately dressed in light tan suiting sharply tailored to fit his athletic form like a glove. His dark eyes beneath level brows narrowed at her between black lashes. There was a quality of strength and vitality about his alien look, a kind of censure which annoyed even while it intrigued, and she addressed him frigidly.

"*Buenos tardes, señor.* Can I help you?" she said slowly in a mixture of English and Spanish. The man looked well educated and her Spanish was restricted. She was not giving him the opportunity of curling his lip and looking down that long aristocratic nose at her mistakes.

"*Buenos tardes, señorita,*" he replied suavely. He spoke in deep cultured tones, taking his time as he looked at her flushed face, tumbled hair and over-bright eyes. "I would say you are the one in need of help. May I ask what you

35

are doing here?"

His English was as faultless as she knew it would be. It was also well chilled as he stood striking an open palm with driving gloves which he clasped in his other hand.

She lifted a small chin defiantly, goaded by his cold regard, his hauteur.

"I might ask the same of you, *señor*. Will you please state your business? I'm busy."

He raised a dark brow maddeningly. "So I observe. Doing men's work, *señorita*? Where is Paco, and why is the garden in a state of neglect?" He looked around him, frowning heavily, his dark eyes eventually taking in the bird table and marble seat, the theme of her labours. Finally, his lips thinned as he looked down on the secateurs on the garden seat. "What exactly is going on here?"

Once more his eyes were on her face. His jaw came into prominence and her heart filled with misgiving. But she collected herself to ask firmly,

"What authority have you to ask that question?"

"Allow me to introduce myself," he said coldly. "I am Juan Vicente de Velez y Stebelo. I own the Villa Acacia."

Phew! Gingerly, Dionis wiped a trickle of perspiration from the side of her nose with a shaking finger. So much for Angela's assurance that this Spanish autocrat and herself would never meet. What a name! What a man! They matched perfectly.

"I beg your pardon," she said. "I understood you were away." The pain in her temples was now acute and she longed to lift her hand to shield her eyes from the hurtful glare. Apparently it did not affect him in the least. He was accustomed to it. His deep tan had been painlessly acquired. He continued to flick the palm of his hand with his gloves, allowing his eyes to flicker over her again probingly.

"I came to see Señor Antonio Alba Terino to whom I let this villa. He also acts as one of my agents and, as I have not heard from him for some time, I am here to find out why. You are a guest here?"

36

"No. I am here at the *señor*'s request to modernize this villa."

He looked startled, so startled that he stopped flicking his gloves to grip them with both hands.

"Please define modernize," he demanded in icy tones.

"I'm an interior decorator," Dionis replied laconically.

His regard was nothing short of contemptuous. "I understood interior decorating to be a man's job. It is hardly a woman's vocation."

Dionis had the feeling of being relegated to the status of a Russian serf. Again she lifted her head, wishing that it would not throb so painfully. The red streaks inside her lids flashed again frighteningly.

"It's a perfectly respectable career for a woman, I assure you. I do the planning and carry out the light jobs myself. I engage workmen to do the heavier ones."

"You surprise me. You have the delicate look of one needing protection. You are certainly not fitted for this type of work. But this is beside the point. If you have been inside the villa you will be aware that it has only recently been decorated throughout."

"It did occur to me," she said inadequately.

He waved his gloves contemptuously to take in the garden. "I presume this is also your province."

Dionis moved uncomfortably. It was growing apparent with each embarrassing moment that this Spanish nobleman or whatever he was had no idea of Antonio's intentions. Perspiration oozed from her afresh as she endeavoured to explain.

"No, it is not. As a matter of fact, Paco has been incapacitated by an injured knee. He started work again only this morning and will be returning after his siesta."

He made a gesture of distaste. "Then will you kindly explain, *señorita*, why you are doing his job?"

"The explanation is perfectly simple and Paco is in no way to blame. I was enchanted by a glimpse of this delightful garden seat and the bird table and I couldn't wait to see what they were really like beneath the tangled undergrowth."

She gave a brief smile in an effort to lighten the oppressive atmosphere. When he ignored it, she flashed him a hostile look from beneath her lashes, thinking that too was unlikely to penetrate his formidable front. Angela's fiancé was lucky not to be within range of those long sinewy brown hands which looked to be as capable of gripping his throat as they now gripped the driving gloves. She quivered inwardly, thinking of all the furniture stored aloft, and hoped to keep him from seeing it until she was sure none of it was damaged. Help was at hand, although it was dearly to her cost. There was a sudden singing noise in her ears, the sun became a guided missile making straight for her face and she stifled a moan as blackness engulfed her.

Everywhere was bathed in a reddish glow when life flowed again in her limbs. Her eyelids weighed a ton, or so it seemed as she lifted them. She was half sitting, half lying in the circle of strong arms. A cool hand was on her burning forehead and she was feeling so sick and ill she was glad of his support.

"How do you feel, *señorita?*" he asked, one hand, remarkably gentle, pushing the damp tendrils of hair from her damp forehead.

But Dionis did not answer. She had never felt so ill in her life. The blackness was coming back again with a deepening of the red glow behind her eyelids.

Gently, he lowered her back against the seat and withdrew his arm.

"Keep still," he said quietly. "I'm going to open the car door."

He was back almost immediately to lift her gently in his arms and she knew no more.

CHAPTER III

Dionis opened her eyes to a strange room. The pain in her head dulled her faculties. But she could see there was beauty in the room, the cool beauty of delicately lovely furniture and colours. A lacquer dressing table handsomely inlaid matched a small writing bureau, two pretty chairs elegantly shaped and beautifully upholstered, a tall vase of flowers, a silver bowl of fruit on the bedside table, Dionis glimpsed these things through a maze of pain as a nurse moved silently towards her. She bent over her in concern.

"How are you? Rotten, I know. Sunstroke can be decidedly painful even in a mild form," she said, English in her speech and in her appearance. She wore a neat little frilled cap on her nut-brown hair and was short, rather thick-set but shapely in her uniform. She had brown eyes, a rather snub nose and a generous mouth. Before Dionis could answer she was pouring out something into a glass from a bottle on the bedside table. Then, very capably, she lifted Dionis gently on her pillows and tipped the contents of the glass down her parched throat.

It was a relief to lie back again on her pillows. Sunstroke, the nurse said.

Dionis had never known such pain. Waves of colour advanced and retracted beneath her eyelids. There was a brief confusion of wandering in dark places before everything was mercifully blotted out. The last thing she remembered was something cool being placed on her hot forehead.

She opened her eyes again to the murmur of voices. A man stood at the side of her bed smiling down upon her benignly. Around forty, he had bushy eyebrows and a wise look.

"How are you feeling, *señorita*?" he asked, standing broad and comforting in the soft light. "I am Doctor Horatio de Quexeri at your service."

"Much better, *gracias*, doctor," she answered, as indeed she was. Her eyes still ached, but the pain in her head had dulled and was bearable. She glanced around the room, aware of the artificial light. "Is it evening?"

"It is ten o'clock," he replied with a smile as he proceeded to lift her wrist in order to take her pulse.

"Oh dear!" Dionis exclaimed. "Señora Lopez will wonder what's happened to me!" It was then that she realized she was wearing a pair of her own pyjamas. Someone must have fetched them from the inn.

"Do not distress yourself, *señorita*. The *señora* has been informed. A day or so in bed will put you right again. And you will be well looked after here at the Villa Jacaranda." The doctor laid down her hand to address someone behind him. "A different kind of quest for you, Don Juan – an English rose among exotic blooms."

Don Juan came forward. His smile had a spontaneous and irresistible charm. Then he was looking analytically at Dionis, his dark eyes full of a curious light.

"You are fortunate that your attack is but a slight one, otherwise you could have been very ill. I trust you will not linger too long in the sun without a hat in the future, Miss Ward."

And let this be a lesson to you, Dionis thought hollowly, for his manner could not have said so more plainly. She quivered at the male element in his voice with its alien intonation. How she resented him, resented his power to rouse an exciting response in her, no more than a vibration at the moment, but it was there – she could not deny it. He was the kind of man who would make his presence felt in any room, dominating it with his air of distinction and arrogant charm. The evening dress he wore was immaculate with no trace of exaggeration anywhere. But she was in his house and some sort of apology was called for.

"I apologize for my thoughtlessness, *señor*," she said. "You have obviously been put to a lot of trouble on my behalf. I'm probably keeping you from your guests at this very moment."

"It is not important," came the cool reply. "What is important is that you will soon be well again."

And from under your well-shod feet, she thought dryly. Aloud, she said,

"I'm grateful for that, since there's no reason why I shouldn't now go back to the inn, where I can take things easy until I've fully recovered."

For a moment the room was still and quiet, full of flowers and soft shaded lights and the cosy atmosphere of rich furnishings. Don Juan lifted his head, and looked strangely feudal.

"I am afraid you will have to reconcile yourself to staying here for the time being. The building alterations at the inn and the noise are not exactly conducive to your recovery. Do you not agree, doctor?"

The doctor smiled down at her kindly. "Of course." He patted her hand as it lay on the counterpane. "Enjoy your convalescence, *señorita*. You will be the envy of *señoritas* for miles round. A pity you do not know any of them. You would have much enjoyment over a cup of chocolate giving an account of your stay beneath the roof of one of our most eligible bachelors."

His words were teasing, his manner easy enough for Dionis to give a light reply. And, although the thought of staying beneath Don Juan's roof filled her with dismay, she managed to say airily, "I shall be able to tell my friends about it when I return home."

She liked the doctor in the well-worn dark suit which proclaimed his calling as quietly and as unobtrusively as the impression he gave of confidence and kindness.

"And make some young Englishman jealous?" he scoffed.

"Perhaps," she answered, aware of the dark still figure by the doctor's side.

"You will have your little joke, *amigo*," Don Juan said. "You will be calling again tomorrow?"

"I shall be here, although your little English nurse seems fully competent." He picked up his small bag. "*Adios, señ-*

orita. Sleep well with no more pain. Delighted to have met you."

Don Juan, his shoulders square and erect, walked with the doctor to the door with the easy grace of an athlete. He could not be more than thirty, Dionis mused as the door closed behind them. He might even be in his twenties and matured beyond his years by his experience and education. She fell to wondering how he had known she was staying at the inn and how she came to be wearing her own pyjamas. She could only surmise that Paco had arrived at the Villa Acacia as Don Juan was driving away in his car, and with that remarkable insight of his, had made a few hurried enquiries. The result was that Paco had been dispatched to the inn to tell Señora Lopez what had happened and to bring the pyjamas back with him to the Villa Jacaranda. He had not taken her to the inn because he thought the *señora* had enough to do with the alterations there. How sickening that this should have happened, and all through her own carelessness. Dionis lay back with closed eyes.

"May I come in?"

The sweet-accented voice in English fell pleasantly upon her ears. Lifting her head from the pillow, Dionis saw a lovely Spanish young woman hovering in the doorway.

She said, "Please do."

The newcomer entered. She was small, dark and about twenty years old. Her black evening dress had bands of velvet round the full skirt and the only note of colour was in the scarlet scarf encircling her slender throat. Long diamond ear-rings matched the jewelled scarf pin winking in the light with every movement and a ring flashed on her hand as she lifted a finger to red lips. Dionis smiled conspiratorially. It was an effort, for she could not have felt less like receiving visitors. Her head was too muzzy and it was far too much trouble to concentrate. But this lovely creature with her tiny feet, trim ankles and lovely expressive hands was really bewitching. Her skin bloomed like a ripe peach and her small laugh like tinkling bells brought dimples into play as she walked gracefully across the room as though to music.

"Welcome to the Villa Jacaranda, Miss Dionis Ward," she said in a delighted whisper. "I am Rosalba Maria de Velez y Stebelo, Juan's sister. My brother tells me you have come from Inglaterra and I am dying to meet you. But you are ill, and I am sorry."

"And so you should be. It was for precisely that reason that I forbade you to come to this room, Rosalba. Please go."

Rosalba swung round as Don Juan entered the room. Her lovely mouth pouted mutinously as she met his stern gaze.

"But, Juan, I only wanted to see the English *señorita* . . ."

"You have seen her. Now go!" he commanded.

For a moment it seemed that Rosalba hesitated. Then the proud dark head inclined graciously towards Dionis. *"Buenas noches, señorita.* I trust that you will enjoy a good night and that you will soon recover."

She drifted from the room like a lovely ghost. Dionis, gazing tenderly after her, met her brother's dark eyes.

"I apologize for my sister's curiosity and lack of good manners," he said formally. "She is a minx." The thin mobile mouth lifted at the corners, but only for a moment. Then he was across the room to look down on her pale face and shadowed eyes. "The doctor says it is possible that you have slept off most of your attack, although the after-effects could linger for a day or so. Nurse is bringing you some refreshment and then you will be left alone to rest. Nurse will stay within call during the night in case you need her."

His voice was kind, but his manner was impersonal. Dionis tried to infuse warmth into the pale smile she gave him, finding his steady regard too unsettling for words.

"You're very kind," she said. "If I've slept most of the trouble away then you can't object to my returning to the inn in the morning."

He digested this with a slight smile which she fancied was tinged with mockery.

"I think not," he replied after a pause. "I would have to put the Villa Acacia out of bounds for a while if you did in order to protect you from your own impulsive actions."

He turned as nurse entered with a covered tray. "Ah, here is Nurse. *Buenas noches*, Miss Ward. Sleep well after your refreshment."

The dark eyes fastened on her own with a glitter which compelled her to capitulate against her will. He had a few words with the nurse in a low voice, then closed the door silently behind him. Dionis had soup, which was the only thing she felt inclined to swallow, and it was not long before she was asleep. She awoke to the glow of morning light filtering through the closed shutters. She had slept all through the night, a dreamless sleep which had refreshed her surprisingly. No pain lurked in her temples and her eyes when she blinked them felt clear and bright. She had a yearning to dip her face into cool water and revel in the pleasure of bending a head free from pain. All was quiet when she left her bed to go beneath the shower. She had combed her hair and was back in bed feeling ready for anyone who appeared when the nurse arrived with her breakfast tray.

"You're awake, I see," was her greeting as she carried the tray to the bed. "How are you this morning? Feeling like breakfast, I hope?" She placed the tray across Dionis's knees and smiled at her cheerfully. "You look much brighter.

"I feel it – in fact there's no reason why I should stay. It's so uncalled-for to have you here when you could be nursing someone who is really ill," Dionis replied firmly, warming to the nurse's friendly smile.

"But, my dear, you're not keeping me from nursing someone else. I just happened to be available when you needed me." She glanced meaningly at the chair beside the bed. "Mind if I stay while you eat? I've already breakfasted."

"Take a seat," Dionis said affably.

The nurse sat down, taking knitting from her apron pocket, a tiny white shape on short knitting needles. "Bootee," she said laconically. "I'm here on a visit to my sister Doris. She and her husband, Felipe Alpurro, are housekeepers here in the Villa Jacaranda. Felipe's family have been in the service of Señor de Velez y Stebelo's family for generations. Don Juan had no idea how ill you were yesterday when he carried you in from his car. You might have been toiling all day in the hot sun and then, of course, the sunstroke would have been very severe. So he asked me to look after you. I suppose he thought my being English would help you better than someone Spanish whom you couldn't understand. I'd do anything for him. I absolutely adore him."

Dionis bit into a fresh buttered roll and watched the knitting needles fly.

"I understood Don Juan spent most of his time at his other residences in Cadiz and Castellon," she said curiously.

"He does. It's quite unusual for him to stay here long, much less have visitors at this time of the year unless he has business with his agents. If his other residences are as nice as this, he's a very lucky man. Each time I come here the Villa steals a little more of my heart. I simply adore Spain – the leisurely long days, the smiling sunlit faces, the music and song and the underlying passion which an Englishman would scoff at but which really exists all the same." She sighed as she counted her stitches. "Take Don Juan, for instance. He has everything, a body like an Adonis, charm and magnetism, is a real man and a gentleman to boot. He's also an Olympic yachtsman, holds a Karate black belt, flies his own plane and is perfectly splendid on horseback. He's the answer to every woman's dream and makes me weak just to think about him. What wouldn't I give to be young and beautiful!"

Dionis laughed. "You speak like someone with one toe in the grave."

The nurse looked surprised. "Do I? I don't feel ancient, especially when I see Don Juan's dark smouldering eyes. I've never known what it is to be beautiful with enough magnetism and charm to attract the opposite sex. The Stebelos have everything, including good breeding and wealth."

45

"Wealth isn't everything." Dionis drank her coffee.

"I agree. But it has a lot of influence. For instance, I'm here on an extended leave, thanks to Don Juan's influence. Doris, my sister, is expecting her first baby. It's overdue and she's very nervous about it. She wants me here when it happens. When Don Juan heard about it he contacted the Matron at the hospital in London where I'm a Sister. The result was that she agreed to extend my leave. I'm thrilled to be able to be here when the baby arrives. I'll have nostalgic moments, though, wishing the baby were mine."

"You can marry and have babies of your own."

The nurse lowered the knitting into her lap and stared down at it. "I'll not be as fortunate as my sister. She's lovely and, like you, she can manage to look interesting even when she's ill." She cast an appraising eye over the delicate texture of Dionis's skin, admiring the long lovely eyes. "Those violet shadows beneath your eyes add to your appeal. If I had them I should look perfectly ghastly. I used to look awful after a spell of night duty at the hospital." She sighed and picked up her knitting and Dionis looked at her averted profile, the brown hair scraped back into a tight bun to accommodate the nurse's cap, the rather snub nose and deep chin. As though conscious of her scrutiny, the nurse looked up to meet her gaze, surprising Dionis by the beauty of her brown eyes between thick stubby lashes.

"You're well on the way to being good-looking," Dionis said cheerfully. "It only needs a bit of effort. As most men notice a woman's eyes and legs you'd do well to concentrate on those. Your eyes are lovely." She put her head on one side, picturing the nurse's face softened by an aura of hair. "Have your hair styled and use a brightening rinse. Change your flat-heeled shoes for court shoes with a medium heel. They would be just as comfortable and ten times as smart as those flatties you wear. Your legs, like your eyes, are your best feature."

The nurse lifted a slim leg to survey her feet ruefully. "I take size fives and wear low heels for comfort. I'm dead on my feet most days at the hospital."

"You're not at the hospital now," Dionis said firmly. "Your feet might be long, but they're slim and would look more elegant in court shoes. Besides, you have a high instep, so you do really need a moderately high heel to give some support."

The nurse appeared to be looking at her feet with new eyes. "You know, you have something there," she said brightly. "Thanks, Miss Ward. I'll see what I can do about it."

"My name is Dionis."

"And mine is Joan — Joan Ford." Nurse Ford grimaced ruefully. "Not a very romantic name, like Rosalba de Velez y Stebelo."

"Don Juan's sister?"

"Yes. She's dark, luscious and lovely. They're a beautiful family." She wrinkled her snub nose. "I don't like that friend of hers, Dolores de Liscondo. She won't be pleased to hear of Don Juan carrying you up to this room from his car. She's certainly got her sights set on him as a husband."

Dionis used her table napkin. "I'm surprised the man is still single. Don't they arrange marriages in Spain anymore?"

"Don Juan was betrothed to a younger sister of Dolores years ago. The marriage was to have taken place when Don Juan reached the age of twenty-five, but a series of incidents prevented it from taking place. In the end Don Juan's *novia* decided he was not for her and went to live with a wealthy aunt in Madrid. She has since married a diplomat there."

"What kind of mishaps prevented the marriage?" Dionis asked curiously. "Don Juan doesn't strike me as a man who would let anything get in his way."

"To begin with, Don Juan lost his parents. They were killed when the horse taking them in their carriage to church bolted. Then Don Juan's *novia's* father died."

"So his fiancée went away to leave the coast clear for her elder sister Dolores. Is she beautiful too?"

"Most Spanish women are," Joan Ford said without rancour. "They're so essentially feminine, which is all to

47

their advantage since most of them tend to run to obesity later in life. Mind you, I think a beautiful Englishwoman is hard to beat." She gave Dionis an appraising look. "You for instance, are everything I wanted to be, with those red lights in your luxurious hair, your slim build, pretty legs and long lovely eyes – the exact opposite to me."

Dionis smiled. "Stop belittling yourself! Men usually prefer women with personality and sex appeal as a partner. You have both."

Joan Ford beamed. "You've made my day! Now I'll have to do something about myself." She cast an experienced eye over the breakfast tray. "Can't you eat any more?"

"I've enjoyed what I've eaten. What time do you think the doctor will arrive?"

Joan Ford pocketed her knitting and lifted up the tray. "Probably before the morning surgery." Her head turned towards the door as someone knocked. "I wouldn't be surprised if that isn't him now."

It was. He came in, took Dionis's temperature, asked the same questions as he had done the previous evening and clasped her hand in parting. He had listened, a line of perplexity between the thick brows, when she had asked for permission to go back to the inn.

"Certainly, if that is what you want. Señora Lopez is a good provider and I can see you are aching to leave this bed. I have dined at the inn on various occasions. Go by all means, but you must rest for several days and keep out of the sun. *Adios, señorita.* We shall meet again."

"He's a nice man," Joan Ford said, when the doctor had gone. "Doctor Horatio de Quexeri. I love these Spanish names. They're so romantic."

Dionis said impishly, "Do you fancy being called Señora Quexeri?"

Joan Ford coloured furiously and laughed as she again made for the door with the tray. "Get away with you!" she exclaimed. "First you try to glamorize me, then you set about getting me a husband. What about yourself? Don Juan is still a bachelor."

"Thanks. But I wouldn't have Don Juan Vicente de Velez y Stebelo for all his wealth. I like Doctor Quexeri. He's less complicated and a perfect pet. So get cracking with that glamour before it's too late," Dionis chuckled.

"The doctor appears to be in great demand."

The deep mocking voice with its alien intonation struck Dionis's heart like a gong. Don Juan was standing in the doorway surveying them both with a narrowed gaze. Dionis flushed to the roots of her hair, wondering how much he had heard of their conversation. His manner gave nothing away. To her instantly alert senses, his lazy air belied the ironic smile hovering on his lips, making her disturbingly aware of him. He really was a very attractive and disturbing personality. She could have hugged Nurse Ford for her blithe acceptance of his presence. Her blush was for the man himself, for his magnetism and charm which she had admitted he had in abundance. His imperious rap on the door had gone unnoticed in their laughter.

Nurse Ford reached the door with her tray. *"Buenos dias,* Don Juan," she said. "The doctor has just left."

"Buenos dias, nurse. I have seen him," was the smooth reply. He stood aside for her to pass through the doorway and Dionis longed to call her back for moral support.

"Buenos dias, Miss Ward." He strode across the room to the foot of the bed. "I believe you are feeling much better." There was an odd little smile on his lips and she felt a strange undercurrent of actual dislike flowing between them.

She gathered scattered wits. "Yes, I am. I'm very grateful for your hospitality. You've been more than kind."

"Yet you cannot wait to get away." He continued to look at her steadily and to her annoyance she found herself blushing as vividly as Nurse Ford. But not for the same reason. She did not like the man. He was far too superior and discerning. While he would be as relieved as she was to know she was leaving, it was the manner of her going which he disapproved of. Having a guest so eager to leave his villa was a new experience for Don Juan Vicente de Velez y

49

Stebelo, and one he did not care for.

"There's no point in my staying," she argued. "I've recovered sufficiently not to need the care of a nurse and there's no reason why I shouldn't return to the inn."

His face had hardened and his expression chilled her. "You are far too independent, Miss Ward. A day or so here at the villa would have acclimatized you gently to the heat and you could have returned to resume work on the Villa Acacia with renewed vigour. However," the wide shoulders lifted arrogantly, "since you prefer to leave now there is nothing more to be said. While I appreciate your eagerness to get back to work I am sure you can find the time to look over the Villa Jacaranda with me before you leave. We will take it gently." An odd little gleam came into his dark eyes, tinged with mockery. "Who knows? You might possibly find inspiration in our antiquated décor."

The gesture was so unexpected, Dionis was startled, and looked it. She hardly liked the crack about the décor, but she could hardly blame him. She would have felt the same in his position.

Her smile was very demure. "I'm always willing to learn. If you will give me ten minutes, I shall be happy to see around the villa."

He was waiting for her at the foot of the fine staircase. Dionis looked down on the tanned rather austere features, saw the momentary gleam of white teeth and felt her face again grow hot. She was as bad as Nurse Ford at blushing at the man, she told herself irritably. The blush receded as he conducted her around.

It was, he explained, a seventeenth-century villa built in the Catalan style. The rooms, high-ceilinged and superbly designed, were ostentatiously beautiful. Dionis looked round with lively interest, noticing how the lace-like alabaster moulding and intriguing mosaics of the ceilings contrasted against the plain walls.

"The Moorish influence accounts for that," he said when she commented on it. "Whenever they reclined, the Moors always lifted their eyes to the heavens. So their artistic talents were concentrated upon the ceilings."

Gazing upwards, Dionis pictured virile, handsome, swarthy Moors lying on their backs admiring the décor of the ceiling as they would a beautiful woman. It occurred to her as she looked that the Moorish influence was still predominant in the Spanish people. Don Juan with his expressive dark eyes and mobile sensitive nostrils would have looked the part when dressed in the flowing robes and fabulous ear-rings of his ancestors. Was he as cruel as they had been? Or had his good breeding toned down that streak in him? He was a Spaniard, nevertheless.

Beauty was the theme throughout the villa – a cool gracious beauty of priceless cabinets gleaming with objets d'art, elegant furniture unique in shape and design exquisitely upholstered in delicately lovely colours, floor vases and pedestals holding flower arrangements, rich rugs, handmade and priceless – all these delights Dionis saw as she walked enthralled beside her host.

With wide enchanted eyes, she looked upon treasures handed down from generation to generation, mellowed but still perfect, untouched by the gentle fingers of time. Through wide-flung doors leading out on to the patio came strange aromatic scents from the gardens.

"It's enchanting!" she breathed, standing motionless on the threshold looking out. Her hair, catching red glints in the sun, framed a vital small face to which only her eyes gave colour. When she had started the tour of the villa, Dionis had felt a trifle embarrassed at the thought of competing with such loveliness with her modern décor. But the uncomfortable sensation had vanished in a genuine wave of admiration at all she saw. Scenes like Goya paintings enchanted and now she was gazing on the beauty outdoors. She smiled and her lips parted to show small pearly teeth. "Everything is so beautiful, and now this!" she exclaimed, gazing at the morning light spreading itself over deep awnings and jalousies protecting windows and patios from the heat of the sun. In the sleepy silence trees stood out starkly against the blue sky and purple creepers cascaded down the white walls of the villa.

"You like it?" he asked her.

She turned sparkling eyes to see him leaning negligently against the door, hands in pockets, level dark brows lifted query-wise, watching her.

"It's fabulous! Earlier you implied that the *décor* might provide me with a few ideas for the Villa Acacia. You were right." She gestured towards the grounds with a slim expressive hand. "The contrast of violent and exciting colour will be my theme for the Villa Acacia."

"And will your designs live and breathe like the Villa Acacia's former décor?"

"In a way. They'll certainly harmonize with the surroundings!"

He said no more but led her outside to the patio. "I trust you have no designs on the grounds of the villa," he said with a hint of satire.

Against the texture of his white cuff, his hand was brown and firm on her elbow as he turned her along the length of the villa. The faint aroma of a freshly groomed fragrance came to her as he walked beside her with an aloof but attentive impartiality. The walled courtyard with its enchanting fountain, the delicately lovely tiles, the flowering trees and shrubs seemed now to be ironically beautiful.

She thought of the smaller courtyard of the Villa Acacia and the enchanting garden. Then she looked up to find him looking down at her speculatively. She did not like it. The man was making her lose her sense of humour.

"As I said before, I'm an interior decorator. Even if I were an experienced landscape gardener I could never improve upon all the beauty surrounding us. It's a miracle how all this loveliness withstands the test of time."

"One theory could be that the architecture is so much part of the land that it has taken root and is therefore part of it. I like it. The Moors might have been noted for their cruelty, but they left behind them a heritage of beauty which is unsurpassed. It is good that we Spaniards have inherited the appreciation of beautiful things."

"You are pure Spanish, *señor*?"

Dionis looked up at the well-shaped head outlined against the white walls of the villa as they walked. His smile was utterly charming. He gave the impression of being entirely self-sufficient, untouched by lesser important lives such as her own.

"Not entirely," he answered. "I had a great-grandmother who was English. Incidentally, her name was Victoria and she came from Sussex."

She longed to ask him more. But something held her back, a kind of restraint combined with a wish not to become involved with relationships which could only be temporary and, in his case, only superficial. He would remain untouched by it. They were poles apart and it was better for them to remain so. How tragic it would be to fall in love with him! The colour rushed to her pale cheeks at the thought. She avoided his downward listening look to say inconsequently,

"It doesn't show. You look decidedly Spanish."

"Does that dismay you?"

The dark eyes flickered over her. He was handsome and virile in the sharp sunlight, erect and sure of himself.

"Why should it?" she answered flippantly, needled by his look of laconic amusement. "I find the Spanish women delightfully lovely and essentially feminine."

"And the men?"

"Very foreign," she said. The next moment she was uttering a cry of delight at the sight of a tall urn set in a corner of the courtyard overflowing with flowers. Her laughter bubbled up at him like a spring. "Forget-me-nots! My favourite flower. May I?" She ran forward and with a beautiful graceful gesture cupped the falling sprays to inhale their fragrance.

He joined her, amused at her rapture. "Allow me."

She straightened and he gathered the delicate flowers into a neat little posy. Dionis gave him a swift look of surprise, then held out her hands like a child when he gave her the flowers.

"Would you not have preferred roses?" There was a teasing quality in his voice which affected her strangely.

"No, thanks." She looked down at them tenderly.

"Are you always so easily pleased, Miss Ward?"

"But they're my favourite flowers." Her eyes met his levelly. "Surely it's the simple gifts in life which give the most pleasure?"

"You have a garden at home?"

"No. My sister and I share a flat."

They had walked to the end of a villa where a wrought iron gate was set in a high stone wall leading round to the back gardens. Through the iron tracing, Dionis could see immaculately laid out grounds beyond where a fountain played in the sun

An old man was trundling a barrow of compost away from them towards the orchards beyond and the air was thick with the perfume of flowering shrubs and trees. Don Juan opened the gate for Dionis to go through, but she was so intent on the beauty of the gardens that she failed to see the step. She stumbled and would have pitched headlong had not his arms whipped out to haul her back against him. The unexpected contact with his lean strong body startled her more than the actual tumble. Excitement raced through her veins like a consuming fire and her heartbeats threatened to choke her. Now, now, she upbraided herself, it's only the reaction at being saved from a nasty fall.

"Sorry," she murmured on regained breath, aware that he could feel the deep throbbing of her heart as he held her against him. "I ought to have looked where I was going. Thanks, *señor*. You saved me from a nasty fall."

"No harm done," he said equably, retaining his hold to give her time to recover.

Dionis wished she could agree with him. It was true as far as he was concerned. Holding her in his arms meant nothing to him. She could feel those years of experience in the strength of him. He was a past master at the game of love, whereas she was only a novice. When he released her Dionis knew he had succeeded in awakening a response in

54

her hitherto unknown in the carefree relationships she had enjoyed with men friends. They walked past the fountain spraying a rainbow of colours in the sun to a shady seat beneath an archway of climbing roses, and because he seemed to expect it, she sat down.

"How is the head? You are feeling well enough to go?" he asked quietly, intent on her bowed head.

"I'm quite recovered, thanks, *señor*," she replied, surprised she was still clutching the posy of forget-me-nots in her hand despite her tumble.

"I still say those forget-me-nots should have been roses," he murmured, reaching up to the arch above her head. The next moment he was offering her a flower, his eyes filled with a curious light.

"Thank you, *señor*," she said, looking at the crimson velvet petals of a half-opened rose.

Her heart gave a curious lurch at the touch of the lean fingers brushing against her own and her eyes fell from his. She was very conscious of herself and of him, the more so because of the silence which followed as he sat down nonchalantly beside her in the opposite corner of the marble seat. He disturbed her; she could feel his presence even when she was not looking at him.

His next remark startled her profoundly. "What exactly are your plans for the Villa Acacia?"

Dionis hid her discomfiture well. The last thing she had expected or wanted was to have to explain her intentions to the owner of the villa. Normally, she could have done so quite easily, but Don Juan's voice was redolent of disapproval before she began. Dionis had taken it for granted that her sister's and Antonio's ideas coincided with each other's. Don Juan was different. His ideas would only coincide with one other, his own.

"I have a letter from Don Antonio stating that he gives me a free hand in redecorating the villa," she told him. "It's to be done throughout in modern décor. My sister Angela prefers it to be modernized before they marry."

"This idea of Don Antonio having a *novia* is extremely

puzzling to me. I have never known him go so far in his affairs before, especially when he is not free."

"What . . . do you mean?" she stammered.

The stilted question came from her lips, but Dionis felt someone else had spoken them. He was frowning now as if there was really something he did not understand.

"Simply that the man is not free to choose a second *novia*. He is already betrothed to a young Spanish woman in Barcelona."

Dionis went paler than ever. Eyes lowered, she said flatly, "I don't believe it. Antonio is engaged to my sister Angela. She has gone to join him in Bermuda, and they plan to marry."

Her fiery glance saw dark eyebrows lifted enlightening like a careful insult and she longed to slap his face. "It's not what you think," she said cuttingly. "My sister is a decent young woman and is not in any way promiscuous. They will be in separate rooms."

"Spare me the details," he said icily. "I have no confirmation of this engagement, nor have I been consulted about these alterations to the Villa Acacia."

Dionis tried to assume a cool indifference, an herculean feat beneath the smouldering gaze of his dark eyes. "Antonio could have written to you. I believe you flit about from one residence to another, so the letter could easily have gone astray."

"Have you met Don Antonio?"

"No, I have not."

"Then you will have no idea what kind of a man he is."

She lifted a chin militantly. "On the contrary. My sister assures me he's a good-hearted young man, and I take her word for it. She's far too clever and discerning to be taken in by a rogue."

"Exactly." The deep voice vibrated on a thread of steel.

"What do you mean, *señor?*" Dionis flashed as anger mounted.

"I believe your sister paid a brief visit here a short while ago." His mouth lifted cynically. "What I heard of that

56

visit was not favourable."

Dionis felt the hot blood rush beneath her skin, lending a sparkle to the long hazel eyes. Her small nostrils dilated. The strain of the last week had pushed her control beyond the limit. With a burning sense of injustice and a hurt which brought the threat of tears, she blazed :

"How dare you judge a person you have never even seen ?"

He returned her fiery gaze unperturbed. "I am merely doing what you have done. You have not met Don Antonio, yet you take your sister's word that he is a good-hearted man. I have done the same regarding your sister."

Dionis was trembling. Her head began to ache and she felt sick and fed up with the whole venture. But if Angela had deceived her, she was still her sister, and no one was going to get away with insulting her. His face was set in a bronze mask. He looked so formidable, so sure of himself that her heart quivered.

"I demand to know what you have been told about Angela," she said shakenly.

He answered laconically as she knew he would. "What I have heard convinces me that they both deserve each other."

This is hopeless, she thought, looking at him appalled. It was like trying to get through a brick wall. The intensity of feeling made speech for the moment impossible and she could only stare at him like a bewildered child. She looked down at the flowers in her hand as he leaned back in his seat surveying her coolly. It was evident that he looked on Angela as some kind of an adventuress and probably looked on herself as such too. What he thought about herself was irrelevant. But she was going to put him right about Angela. No one was going to belittle any member of her family unjustly and get away with it !

"I think I can give you a much truer picture of my sister Angela than any casual acquaintance," she began in a strange detached voice hardly recognisable as her own. "To begin with, she's a decent hard-working young woman who

57

is merely rather foolish in her love affairs. She's a buyer in a fashionable West End store in London where she is held in high esteem. I can assure you she's no adventuress. She has been engaged to no less than two millionaires and broken off the engagements herself."

Outwardly he appeared to be in no way impressed. Sitting negligently in his corner, he drummed flexible fingers on the arm of the seat and surveyed her calmly.

"Don Antonio is a long way from being a millionaire, or even a man of means." he said dryly.

"I know nothing about that. The only thing which concerns me is that my sister might be in love with him." Dionis raised eyes from which the sparkle had gone. "I have to take that chance."

By now her head was throbbing and the urge to get away was almost unbearable. Her face was rigid, a pale mask in which her eyes burned beneath levelled brows.

"I am sorry, but I do not share your optimism over this affair," he said at last. "I am inclined to be rather cynical regarding this true love business." His eyes narrowed at her exhausted look. "However, I suggest you go back to the inn and rest. I trust you will be sensible and take the full siesta each day."

Instantly, Dionis was on her feet to walk beside him to the courtyard where the sun shone on the long body of the car. He opened the door and helped her into the front seat, saying, "Your night clothes will be laundered and sent to the inn."

Dionis made no reply. Against such callous indifference, there was nothing she wanted to say. The journey was made in silence and eventually the big car swung into the courtyard of the inn. It was her intention to slip out of her seat before he could come round to her door. In her anxiety to be gone, she fumbled with the lever and the door remained closed despite her efforts.

He said curtly, "Before you go, Miss Ward, I would like the keys to the Villa Acacia, please."

Dionis gave him a wide-eyed incredulous gaze. "I beg

58

your pardon," she said.

He held out a lean hand. "The keys, please," he repeated. "Do not look so shattered. I only wish to make sure that you rest and are fully recovered before you commence work there. We can discuss your work there when you are more fit."

She was shattered. She had expected opposition from him, but nothing so high-handed as this. The urge to throw in her hand and steer clear of the whole business was strong until she thought of Angela. She had to be loyal, and in antagonizing Don Juan, she was doing her sister a great wrong. After all, he had the last word about the villa, and Angela's fiancé was also a distant relative. The sense of conflict between them had to be swept aside. If Don Juan's tenants could find the lighter side to his nature, then he must have one. She would never find it by being openly aggressive. Opening her handbag, she took out the keys and dropped them in his hand.

"*Gracias,*" he said, dropping them into the pocket of his jacket. Then he was leaning over her to release the catch on the door. In her haste to be away she caught the hand holding the flowers against the side of the doorway and scattered them in all directions. Simultaneously, they bent to pick them up. Whether by accident or design, Don Juan's foot obliterated the rose and squashed it flat. He looked at her swiftly, but she kept her eyes on the flowers now intact in her hand. Her voice was barely a whisper when she thanked him and went swiftly indoors.

Señora Lopez greeted her as she entered, eyeing her pale face and worn look anxiously. "How are you, Miss Ward? Better, I hope. We were so sorry to hear about your collapse, but happy to know you were in good hands."

"I'm quite recovered but for a tiresome headache." Dionis smiled wanly. "I never have headaches as a rule. I shall probably feel better tomorrow."

While she spoke, Dionis was on the alert for the sound if Don Juan's car. It came as she finished speaking and she heard him leave with relief. She had never disliked anyone so much in her life.

"We must take more care of you," the *señora* was saying.

Dionis said firmly, "Please don't think any more about it. I shall be all right. I appreciate you having me here at all when you have all the upset of workmen on the premises. You already have enough on your hands without extra work."

"The workmen are not coming for a day or so. Don Juan's orders until you are quite well again. The alterations are temporarily postponed. I also have to make sure you do not go out into the sun for the next two days."

Dionis stared in dismay. "But it isn't necessary for Don Juan to be so high-handed. I can keep out of the sun, but to stop the workmen . . . it's ridiculous!"

The *señora* shrugged. "It is entirely Don Juan's concern, since we rent the inn from him. The alterations are being carried out under his directions. He is a clever and astute man with an eye on the future when there will be more and more tourists coming this way. Don Juan is a very kind and considerate man and we all love him. Now, if you are going upstairs to rest, I will bring you a cool drink."

So the *señora*, like the inhabitants of the surrounding farms, was under the jurisdiction of Don Juan, Dionis mused, going slowly and thoughtfully upstairs. She recalled the short journey to the inn with the big car slowing down when it neared farm entrances where a farmer's wife and sometimes the farmer working with his men acknowledged him courteously. Their dark-complexioned faces had eased into smiles of genuine warmth and affection when Don Juan had driven by, lifting a hand accompanied by his charming smile. Dionis entered her room, closed the door and stood for several thoughtful minutes to review the situation as it stood. Her faculties were suddenly numbed by the immensity of her task. Hitherto the course she had taken had been utterly unknown to her. Undisputedly, she had taken the job of her own accord, but she did not feel that the choice had been wholly hers. It seemed that from now on she also would be under the supervision of Don Juan, who heartily disapproved of her to begin with. Dionis put the small posy of forget-me-nots he had given her into a small glass vase of water and wondered about the rose. Had he stepped on it deliberately, regretting his action in giving it to her? He evidently looked upon Angela and herself as a couple of adventuresses, out for what they could get. She pushed slim fingers through hair which felt too heavy for her head. Her temples ached and she hoped fiercely that she was not going to be ill again. Only by keeping fit and on her toes could she be a match for the exasperating, arrogant Don Juan Vicente de Velez y Stebelo.

CHAPTER IV

DIONIS was up the next morning and downstairs to breakfast before Señora Lopez could send up a tray. She took her
place at the little table beneath the lemon trees to the pleasing aroma of freshly baked rolls and coffee coming from the
kitchen quarters. Tercia, swinging gracefully across the
courtyard with the pitcher of milk, was surprised to see her
there. After making the most solicitous enquiries regarding
Dionis's attack of sunstroke, she expressed her delight at
her recovery. She herself would not have been in such a
hurry to leave the Villa Jacaranda and the exciting Don
Juan. He was so *simpatico*, so attractive. Did not Dionis
agree? When Dionis just smiled she went on enthusiastically:

"Everyone is so happy for him to be here. We see so
little of him. Soon we expect to hear that he and Señorita
Dolores de Liscondo are affianced."

Tercia, standing poised with the pitcher of milk on her
shapely hip, bubbling with the joy of living, made an enchanting picture. Her gypsy ear-rings and dark liquid eyes
along with her soft feminine curves and peach-bloom look
gave the impression of her having been brought up barefoot
in a happy, sunlit land. Her behaviour had been disciplined
by loving parents to prepare her for the sweet satisfying role
of wife and mother. Lucky Tercia!

"Tercia, do not gossip about *el señor*. I am waiting for
the milk."

Señora Lopez appeared in the doorway to shrug apolo-
getically at Dionis before following her daughter indoors.
Dionis had to smile. Here like everywhere else the world
over the chief topic of conversation in the feminine com-
unity was men. So Don Juan was on the brink of being engaged to a sultry beauty with the delicious name of Dolores
de Liscondo. Well, good luck to her! She would certainly
need it.

Dionis spent the morning in her room writing letters and catching up with her correspondence. Señora Lopez brought her refreshment mid-morning, enquired how she was feeling and said Don Juan had enquired in a similar vein. Dionis was happy to inform her that she was feeling quite well again and hoped to stay that way. She had apparently slept away her headache of the previous day and was more than thankful. When she went down to lunch there was a letter beside her plate at the small table beneath the lemon trees. The beautiful script was not familiar, so she slipped it into the pocket of her linen dress to read later.

Four German students, who had stopped by for lunch, sat at the next table and spoke to her in perfect English. There were the usual polite exchanges about the weather and the young men talked of their journey through Spain with haversacks on their backs. Between Calpi and Tarragona they had stopped to pick large ripe juicy oranges from the trees by the roadside – it was a recognised custom for passers-by to be allowed to pick them and quench their thirst. Looking Dionis over appraisingly, they enquired politely if she was on holiday. Revelling in their excellent English, she replied diplomatically and said she was there at the invitation of a relative.

The young students, big and blond in their shorts, took their leave after lunch. Dionis imagined them taking their siesta by some cool mountain stream before continuing on their way and promptly forgot all about them. Going to her room, she opened the letter. The heading on the notepaper was in gold lettering, an invitation to dine at the Villa Inez on the occasion of the silver wedding of Don Fernando and his wife Inez. A warm feeling of pleasure brought a smile to her lips at the thought. It would be nice to go out after spending all day at the inn.

Dionis slept through the siesta and awoke feeling refreshed. Opening the shutters of her windows, she breathed in the perfumed fragrance of country air. The shimmering heat of the day had given way to a dry brilliance where trees stood sharply outlined against the blue sky with the distant tinkle of goat bells like fairy music to her ears attuned to city sounds.

A little after six she had tea in the courtyard, where she nibbled delicious little pastries and drank hot chocolate. She had become used to life at the inn, the comings and goings amid shadows, music, laughter and a life rich in its utter simplicity. This evening the air seemed to be full of music. Tercia was singing in the kitchen, a sentimental love song in Spanish, and very faintly Dionis could hear the soft twang of a guitar. The white cat came to rub gently against her legs, then scampered suddenly to the kitchen in response to the *señora's* gentle call. Dionis refused to think at all of Don Juan or Angela and was determined to enjoy her little break away from their demands. She would study her Spanish after tea until it was time to dress to dine with Don Fernando and his wife.

At nine-thirty Don Fernando's little horse and carriage arrived, and with the delicate pink chiffon skirt of her evening dress held high above her silver slippers, Dionis ran downstairs. Agustín, a large thick-set man, who did odd jobs for Don Fernando, helped her up beside him and they set off into a night of breathtaking beauty.

Agustín was the type one usually met in a village – carefree, indifferent to monetary gains, invariably polite and helpful. His natural aptitude for singing on all occasions gave one the opinion that he was a little soft in the head. But to Dionis he was part of this strange and wonderful country. For a while there was no sound save the clip-clop of horses' feet as they sped along beneath a sky alive with stars. Dionis was content to enjoy the beauty of the night, the mysterious shadows broken occasionally by the lights in houses and the nocturnal scents rising on the cooler air. When Agustín's voice lingered softly on a flamenco, Dionis felt it was the perfect touch, bringing a throbbing ecstasy and delight to the beauty of the night. He sang with feeling in Spanish.

"*Gracias,* Agustín. That was lovely," she said when he helped her down at her destination.

The Villa Inez, Don Fernando's home, was a white bel-fried building overlooking a valley. From the open door in the brazier-lit patio came the amiable chattering of guests. Dionis was giving the horse the two lumps of sugar she had remembered to bring when Don Fernando came out to greet her.

"*Buenos noches*, Dionis," he said, greeting her warmly. "I trust you have recovered from your illness."

When she assured him that she had, he stood aside for her to enter the house where she was greeted by his wife.

Doña Inez was petite and gentle in her beautiful high-necked lace blouse and flowing skirt. The fine black lace covering her grey hair framed a face full of character and charm. She greeted Dionis kindly when Don Fernando in-troduced her. As she held out a small white hand her eyes scanned the slender figure in the pink and silver gown, noting the fair skin and long hazel eyes with satisfaction.

"The pain of too much sun has gone, *niña*?" she asked, nodding her head wisely. "You will get used to it, although your lovely fair skin is more enchanting without the tan. I am sure the *señoritas* will look upon it with envy — and I can see you cracking some male Spanish hearts too!" Doña Inez gave an impish smile. "Fortunately, Fernando's heart is long past the cracking stage. Come, I will introduce you to our guests." Her accented English was as delightful as the daintiness of her small hands and tiny narrow feet. Dionis felt the spontaneous warmth of her welcome wrap-ping around her like a cloak. The beautiful room, cool and spacious with its air of faded elegance, held a calm and dignity which beckoned her in. Doña Inez drew her to the first couple who stood chatting together glass in hand. "You are already acquainted with Doctor Horatio, I believe."

Dionis answered politely, acknowledging the doctor, who congratulated her on her swift recovery. Then Doña Inez was speaking again, introducing his companion, a young Spanish woman who could have been in her late twenties. She would have been good-looking but for the small sloping chin which gave her a bird-like appearance.

Her hands were bare of rings, but she had a magnificent diamond brooch at the neck of her high-collared black dress.

Doña Inez said, "My husband's sister, Doña Peralto. Miss Dionis Ward from London.

Dionis looked into dark rather sad eyes. If the woman's manner was reserved, Dionis felt a shy warmth in her greeting. Her black hair, coiled into the nape of her neck, was beautifully smooth and neat and her slightly hooded eyes were made interesting by the thick black lashes. Her nose was short and hooked very slightly. Pity about the sloping chin which, Dionis thought, seemed rather out of place with the rest of her face. Dionis wondered if the woman was interested in the doctor. The soft flush on her face might have been heightened by his presence.

Dionis was introduced to the rest of the guests, who included her host's son and his wife. A servant supplied her with a glass of wine and she found Don Fernando at her side. As they drank their wine, he told Dionis that his son Ruiz had been married a year. He and his wife were expecting their first child. Naturally, he and Doña Inez were delighted. Dionis looked towards the daughter-in-law, a plump, glowing young woman who had the appearance of being fed entirely on peaches and grapes. Her young husband was looking at her very tenderly as they drank as though to each other. Time passed with Dionis mingling with the guests along with Don Fernando. Mechanically counting the guests, she discovered that she was odd man out. The fact made her slightly curious, and when Don Fernando escorted her back to his wife, Dionis had a feeling of anti-climax.

Feeling rather strange, she saw Doña Inez turn and followed her eyes towards the door. Someone had just entered, striding in with his usual exciting male vitality. Dionis stood rooted to the spot as Don Juan Stebelo, in top form both physically and mentally, made straight for his hosts. His unexpected appearance was like a hand imprisoning her heart. But she did not pause to wonder why this man entering the room like a cool mountain breeze should have the power to ruin her evening. She only obeyed the sudden urge to move away until the quivering of her nerves had subsided. The chance came when she moved to a table near the door to put down her empty glass on a tray. It was then that th e guests moved of one accord towards the dining-room.

"*Buenas noches*, Miss Ward. How is the head?"

The cool voice held a smile and Dionis realized with dismay that Don Juan was to escort her in to dinner.

"I'm quite well again, thanks," she replied, adding meaningly, "I hate having to mark time before starting to work again."

"A pity this zest for work has to find an outlet doing someone else's job," he said cynically.

"One learns by experience," she answered, gathering courage with every word. "I am ready any time to discuss the alterations at the Villa Acacia, *señor*."

"In other words you want the keys?" he commented whimsically.

"If you have no objections."

"Rather late in the day for that, wouldn't you say?"

They had reached their places at the table and he seated her before taking the chair to her left. Dionis made no reply. As she picked up her table napkin with shaking fingers it suddenly became imperative for her to do the job. Returning home without tackling it would leave her forever wondering just how versatile she could be on foreign soil. Apart from letting Angela down, there was a stubborn streak in her, a burning desire to show Don Juan that a woman could be as good as a man in interior decorating. Doctor Horatio, taking the seat to her right with Doña Pilar beside him, claimed her attention. When she glanced again at Don Juan he was immersed in conversation with a man on his left. An immaculately dressed cousin of Don Fernando's from Madrid, he appeared to be well informed on world affairs.

Ever conscious of Don Juan's nearness, Dionis gave all her attention to Pilar Peralto and the doctor on her right.

Pilar Peralto had an exceptionally high colour and her nervousness in the doctor's presence was obvious to Dionis, who did her best to draw her out. Inexperienced though she was, instinct told Dionis that poor Pilar was in love with the big kind man by her side and he could not have been less aware of it. All that was feminine in Dionis longed to shake him into that awareness, and by the end of the meal she had the satisfaction of seeing Pilar's colour return to normal.

After dinner, the women went on to the lantern-lit patio where Dionis sat with Doña Inez, her daughter-in-law and Pilar Peralto until the men joined them.

It was then that Dionis escaped into the lantern-lit grounds. She took with her the memory of Pilar looking very attractive with a deep glow of happiness lighting her features when the doctor took Dionis's place beside her. So much for Joan Ford, the little nurse, and their joke about changing her name to that of the doctor. How nice it would be if he did marry Pilar. Unlike Joan Ford, the Spanish woman had little opportunity for meeting suitable males in her inhibited existence. And it would be better for her to marry one of her own kind. There was a difference between the two races of temperament − the English with their cool Saxon strain and the Spanish with their *furia española* or Spanish fury. Again she fell to wondering about Don Juan. How much of that *furia española* was she to encounter in him before her task was done? She had a notion that that icy reserve of his hid volcanic eruptions underneath. A slight movement in the trees reminded her of the huge bird swooping for its prey and Paco's words, skill is better than strength. Quelling a shiver, she thought that Don Juan had both.

The beauty of the garden was something she would not have missed for worlds. Away in the dark blue distance, the hills rose majestically beneath a blue veil of light, deepening to black velvety darkness where it was pricked by the lights of scattered villas or farms. It was like a garden of Eden, for though nothing seemed real, nothing also seemed impossible. Behind her on the patio conversation was laced with laughter, subdued and foreign to her ears. Perhaps she had sensed her own isolation and had escaped of her own accord. But not for long. Someone else was strolling through the garden behind her, someone who was making their presence felt, affecting her physically and mentally in a disturbing fashion.

At last she turned to see Don Juan. The scent of his cigar had alerted her as to his male presence. A lean hand, brown against the white texture of his cuff, lifted to remove the cheroot from his mouth. His deep voice when he spoke vibrated quietly on the still evening air.

"Don Fernando and his guests are gathered on the patio, Miss Ward. They wait to hear the song of the nightingales in the garden. The birds will not sing if anyone is wander-about to disturb them. Will you join us?"

Dionis felt her face go hot. Why did he always have her at a disadvantage? Walking beside him, she was aware of everything about him, his erect nonchalant walk, the faint emanation of his masculine fragrance and his powerful and predominant personality. As they approached the warmly lit patio, the guests looked an alien crowd and Dionis felt their dark gaze upon them both as she left Don Juan's side to take a seat beside Don Fernando.

"Did you enjoy the garden?" he asked politely.

"Very much. The loveliness lured me out," she replied, instantly at ease. "I had no idea of the nightingales singing."

Don Fernando studied the tip of his glowing cigar. "I doubt if you disturbed them. From here you looked like an enchanting moonbeam flitting about in the dark places."

The soft buzz of conversation was flowing again as before, no louder than the muted strumming of a guitar in the far corner of the patio. Gradually conversation dwindled into silence with the guitar being twanged very softly. Then gradually another sound swelled in the silence, the pure trill of liquid notes from feathered throats. The guitar ceased and the nightingales combined their efforts until the beauty of their song mounted to a crescendo of loveliness.

The guests sat or stood silently, lost in their spell. When it was over the warm response still lingered in Dionis's eyes. With soft lips gently parted, she lifted her head to gaze out into the garden, seeking a glimpse of the nightingales, but she looked no further than the brass hanging lamp suspended from the ceiling of the patio as her eyes met the dark glittering ones of Don Juan. For brief electric moments he held her gaze captive before she lowered her eyes. Charmed into forgetting his presence by the liquid notes of the feathered songsters, Dionis was again vitally aware of him. Like several other male guests, he had remained standing to smoke a cigar and was leaning against one of the marble pillars supporting the patio. He had joined in the general conversation, but had not spoken directly to her. Now someone was twanging the guitar again and a pleasing voice sang flamenco softly.

Others followed, all in Spanish, until Don Fernando, moving about among his guests, had a word in the musician's ear. The result was a flamenco song in English for Dionis, who caught Don Juan's mocking smile when it had finished. The party broke up in the small hours with Don Juan keeping himself aloof from Dionis until he was actually taking his leave. Then, to her dismay, he offered her a lift. Her acceptance, coming from a wary heart, was stilted. Don Fernando kissed her hand and she slid into the spacious interior of Don Juan's car, the last guest to depart.

While she had enjoyed the evening and the nightingales, a strange restlessness had invaded her usual calm. Dionis could not define it, but she knew with a quiver that the man sitting so silent beside her accounted for it. As a guest along with him at the Villa Inez, she had felt a sense of equality. There they had been a man and woman meeting on equal terms. Now his silence gave her the feeling of reaching out for something that could never be hers. There was no place for her among these people whose lives had flowed along on tranquil lines long before she arrived and would continue to do so long after she had gone. The young woman from Inglaterra's invasion into their midst would soon be forgotten except by Don Fernando who had known her father.

Don Juan seemed intent on returning her to the inn as swiftly as possible. In no time at all they were turning into the lantern-lit courtyard.

"Tired, Miss Ward?" he asked, opening her door and looking down into her eyes with the intent way he had, and his smile brightened the gloom. "You will become accustomed to keeping late hours and taking the siesta." He paused his hand on her arm. "You are fully recovered from your illness? No head pains or dizziness?"

"Quite recovered, thanks. And thanks for bringing me home."

"It is a pleasure." He helped her from the car and because he seemed to expect it she held out her hand. He took it, gave a half bow, and said, "*Buenas noches*, Miss Ward — sleep well."

Dionis was quite unprepared for the cold metal coming in contact with her hand. Foolishly, she stared down at the keys to the Villa Acacia. He had gone before she could thank him.

Dionis awoke the following morning free of the frustration of the last few days. Her heart leapt with joy at the thought of being able to concentrate on her job at last. Leaving her bed, she took a peep at the forget-me-nots in the vase of water to see if any roots had sprouted on the end of the stalks. Silly of her to expect them yet, but everything seemed possible this morning. She must remember to tell Tercia not to throw them away as she wanted to plant them in a small pot and take them back home with her when the time came for her to go.

When Tercia brought her breakfast at the little table in the courtyard she mentioned the flowers.

"But we have forget-me-nots in the garden at the back of the inn. You can have some with roots to plant in a little pot now if you wish," she exclaimed.

"They wouldn't be the same, Tercia. These were a gift, not something I have asked for."

"Ah!" Tercia waggled a finger knowingly. The Spanish gypsy ear-rings gleamed no less bright than her dancing eyes. "It is an admirer who has given them to you!"

Dionis felt the blush steal up from her neck, but was saved the embarrassment of a reply by the sudden appearance of a middle-aged man of medium height whose form was vaguely familiar. Then she remembered him accompanying Tercia that first evening on her visit to her *novio*. He was her father.

"Tercia," he said on a note of command, "you are not to question the *señorita*." When Tercia had fled back to the kitchen, Señor Lopez gave Dionis an apologetic smile. "Tercia is young and full of romance. You must allow for her inquisitiveness."

Dionis smiled. "I am young and romantic too, Señor Lopez, and I find Tercia is adorable. Already I love her."

He nodded understandingly. "It is good to see you do not take offence. Some Englishwomen visitors I have found cold and austere." His smile made him appear boyish and there was a twinkle in his eyes. "However, we live in hopes that our warm sun will melt them into being human before they leave. Enjoy your breakfast, *señorita*, and your day."

At the Villa Acacia, Paco had obviously been busy while she had been away. Disfiguring weeds had been cleared away, revealing pretty pink and white oleander, bright red jasmine and blue plumbago. Bees were humming their appreciation of a tidy hunting ground among flowers tied back neatly against white walls and terraces. Indoors, Dionis decided that the lovely designed ceilings would look impressive in deep tones of colour against paler walls. A long curved chaise-longue in the lounge would look well with leather and chrome chairs, a really thick carpet in a neutral shade and colourful cushions.

The dining-room would be more austere. For instance, a long oval table and matching chairs covered in melamine in a pastel blue would accommodate the maximum number of guests with comparative ease. The ceiling would be in a warm apricot with charming brass hanging lamps to reflect colourfully on the plain white walls.

At twelve o'clock, pleased with her morning's work, Dionis went outdoors to see a perspiring Paco mopping his brow. He was sitting on the garden seat in the shade of the trees. Beside him was a picnic basket.

"*Buenos dias*, Señorita Ward," he said. "Come, sit down in the shade, for when the sun moves around this seat will be too hot to sit on." He smiled as she obeyed and sat beside him. "You are better, *señorita*? Don Juan was angry that I had not let him know about my knee. He said he could have put someone else on the job while I was indisposed." He gave her a sheepish look. "He blamed me, *señorita*, for your collapse."

"Oh dear, Paco! I'm so sorry, and it was all my fault. I told Don Juan so."

She watched him open a flask from the basket and fill two thick mugs with sparkling liquid.

"Lemonade, *señorita*. My wife makes the finest lemonade in Spain." He handed her one of the mugs.

"*Gracias*, Paco." Dionis drank thirstily, revelling in the cold sharpness in her dry throat. "Hmm, it's very good indeed," she said, lowering the mug to look around the tidy grounds. "You've made a very good job of the garden, Paco, and I appreciate it very much."

Paco drew a hand across his mouth after taking a satisfying drink and looked around unimpressed. "There is still much to be done."

Dionis emptied the mug and gave it back to him. "*Gracias*, Paco. That was lovely." She put on the floppy-brimmed hat she had taken off inside the villa. "I'm going back to the inn now and will leave you to it. I should hate Don Juan to come and find me here at the hottest hour of the day. I shall be back after the siesta." She stood up "Don't work too hard. And take care of the knee. How is it today?"

"Like a discontented wife, always complaining." He

73

grimaced as though with remembered pain. "I ignore it, and soon it will become tired of having no attention and settle down to work without bothering me."

"Like a discontented wife?" she teased, and laughed. Paco laughed too.

The sudden change from grave to gay for which the Spanish people were gifted amused Dionis. She was still smiling when she arrived back at the inn to be met with a delicious aroma from the kitchen quarters as she went up to her room.

"This is good, *señorita*," Tercia said, arriving immediately Dionis sat down at the small table in the courtyard for lunch. "There is chicken with rice and peppers cooked only in the best oil and not too heavily spiced for the English palate."

Dionis sniffed appreciatively as Tercia set down an appetising dish.

"Smells good," she said lightly, turning her head as a young man entered the courtyard carrying a large square box in his arms.

Tercia drifted towards him, lifted the box lid and peered inside. What she saw inside evidently satisfied her, for she nodded her head and gestured towards the kitchen. The young man obeyed, but not before he had flashed his dark eyes at Dionis and whispered something swiftly to Tercia in Spanish. Tercia laughingly shook her head and Dionis saw his cheeky grin before he disappeared into the inn.

Tercia came back to the table to pick up the now empty tray to stand with it on her hip in a typical feminine pose. Her eyes sparkled with fun. "You have an admirer, *señorita*." She shrugged as though in no way surprised. "He is only one of many who have paid you compliments. I refer to the workmen on the alterations at the back of the inn."

"But I've never seen the workmen," exclaimed Dionis in some surprise. "I've only heard them."

"They see you on your way to the Villa Acacia from the roof at the back of the inn where they are working."

74

"Really?" Dionis tried the paella and found it delicious. So even a quiet country inn had eyes! She gazed upwards to the roof of the inn when Tercia had disappeared inside, expecting to see the flashing of teeth and dark eyes. But all was quiet except for a tiny bird peering down at her inquisitively with tiny bright eyes.

CHAPTER V

Dionis dutifully had her siesta and was back again at the villa before Paco had returned. On her way there, she had wondered what treasures were stored among the furniture at the top of the house. One or two items like floor vases, pretty footstools, or screens would blend beautifully with the décor she had in mind. On her way up to the top of the villa where the furniture was stored, Dionis paused to reflect whether Don Juan would care to loan his furniture to the modern décor. Anyway, she argued, she could ask, and using it was much better than having it in store. Opening the door of the store room, she saw a miscellany of furniture and heavy gilt-framed oil paintings. Then her eager gaze alighted upon two floor vases, incredibly lovely in shape and design. How fabulous they would look in the lounge filled with trumpet jasmine! Her enthusiasm dampened a little when she saw they were beneath a rather precarious pile of chairs topped by an exquisite lady's writing desk. The small writing table did not look too secure, but she dared not disturb it in case the whole lot collapsed. However, she was slim enough to crawl in beneath the structure and gently ease out the vases.

Cautiously, she crawled forward on all fours, reached out tentatively for the rim of the nearest vase and eased it gently towards her. Within minutes it was free and she placed it down by the door. The second vase was wedged behind a solid table leg and she had to crawl in still further to reach it. At last, after a great deal of breathless manoeuvring the vase was out. In her delight, Dionis forgot caution and on moving out dislodged the chairs hanging precariously above her head. The pile of furniture swayed ominously and before she could put the vase down there was a crash. For pulsating seconds, Dionis stood holding her prize. It was some time before she put the rescued vase down beside the other to look at the collapsed furniture.

The beautiful little lady's writing table had slipped down between the fallen chairs. Gingerly, she moved forward and her hand flew to her mouth in horror. One of the delicately curved legs was buckled grotesquely, snapped off just below where it joined the table top. With a rasping breath of dismay, Dionis straightened to push back her hair with a trembling hand. This was awful, far worse than anything she had dreamed could happen. What was she to do now? As she leaned back miserably against the closed door, she wished she had never entered the room. What an intolerable situation to be in! Anyone with the scantiest knowledge of antiques could see that the thing was valuable, and her own innate honesty would not allow her to keep silent about it.

Why had she had to be so eager? Then as though one castastrophe was not enough, the sound of voices came from the garden. Oh no, it could not be! But there was no mistaking that deep baritone voice. Holding her breath, Dionis listened.

Don Juan sounded light-hearted. "I will find the *señorita*, Paco. *Gracias*."

With her heart threatening to knock a hole in her ribs, Dionis listened to the light firm footsteps as he searched the downstairs rooms. Those few precious moments gave her time to pull herself together. Leaving the room, she closed the door quietly behind her and went downstairs. She caught him between rooms, hatless and faultlessly attired in a dark suit.

His sudden smile was one of extraordinary charm. His white teeth gleamed.

"Forgive this intrusion," he said politely. "I was passing with my sister and a friend when they expressed the desire to see the Villa Acacia – and you."

He had walked to within feet of where she stood at the foot of the staircase and was immediately frowning at Dionis, who stood petrified, unable to answer. He followed the frown up quickly as was his way and asked with concern, "Are you all right, Miss Ward? You look pale and upset."

Dionis pulled herself together with an effort. His perceptiveness was amazing. She gave a wavering smile. "Yes, thanks, *señor*. My delicate look is deceptive. I'm healthy and quite well."

The pleat between the dark eyes deepened. She had the feeling that he was not altogether satisfied. "Even so," he commented slowly, "I am of the opinion that you have chosen the wrong profession. Something less strenuous, less demanding would have been better in your case."

"But I love my work. I've made a success of it too."

He gave a shrug of distaste. "I would not care for a sister of mine to do such work." His mouth thinned and Dionis caught a glimpse of his virile Moorish ancestors in the cruel set of his mouth as he paused to look around the empty hall. "I see the furniture has been removed, otherwise I am sure you would not have hesitated in tackling part of the job of moving it yourself." He regarded her broodingly. Miserably, it occurred to her that to tell him now of the wrecked writing table would be disastrous. It would only serve to prove his belief that the job was too much for her.

Dionis wrenched her thoughts away from the incident of the writing table to dwell upon Don Juan's sister and her friend waiting outside the villa. And suddenly there they were.

"Ah, Juan ! We wondered what was keeping you."

The words were uttered lightly, seductively in Spanish by a vision of loveliness, one of two young women who appeared in the entrance to the hall. The most dominating of the two, like her companion, was dressed expensively in a model dress of Spanish lace. Her glossy black hair, parted in the centre, framed her pretty face with a disciplined smoothness and was knotted in the nape of her rather long neck. Dark eyes beneath strongly marked brows stared curiously at Dionis and her beautifully shaped mouth drooped a little at the corners at the sight of her figure so slender and sweet, her fair skin in strong contrast to her own olive one showing no flaws in the sunlit empty room.

Don Juan said smoothly, "You have already met my sister Rosalba, Miss Ward."

Dionis smiled as Rosalba came forward with dancing dark eyes. Apart from their dark rich colouring, brother and sister were not very much alike, for Don Juan was so essentially masculine and Rosalba so feminine. They were alike in their mannerisms, Dionis thought. Both had that nonchalant well-bred look, the same way of assessing a person with that faint amused smile, so enchanting in Rosalba, so disturbing in Don Juan.

"I trust you have fully recovered from your illness, Miss Ward," Rosalba said in English.

Dionis replied politely in the affirmative and Don Juan introduced Dolores de Liscondo. He was smiling at the slightly taller woman who came forward in a haughty, withdrawn manner. Dionis, looking at the calm impassive features, felt a strange wariness inside her. After Rosalba's warm greeting, Dolores was as chilly as an east wind.

Dolores followed Don Juan's lead and spoke in educated English. "You must pardon our curiosity, Miss Ward, but when Juan told us about you decorating the Villa Acacia we were frankly curious. I wanted to see the English Amazon who dares to take up a man's profession." The long lashes came down in an attempt at demureness, veiling the surreptitious glance at the slim trousered legs.

Dionis had put on her working attire this afternoon, primrose pants with a matching sleeveless top. She met the derisive curl of the *señorita*'s red lips with a friendly smile. "It's a woman's profession too," she said without rancour.

"But not as yet in Spain, Miss Ward. We Spanish women prefer to leave the more masculine jobs to the men, who like their women to be absolutely feminine."

"But, Dolores, women in Spain are following professions hitherto dominated by men. We already have two very successful women lawyers practising in Madrid. As for being feminine, I find Miss Ward delightfully so," Rosalba said teasingly, and dimpled enchantingly at her brother.

"Do you not agree, Juan?"

Don Juan took his time at looking Dionis over. "Miss Ward is certainly no Amazon, although she is determined to prove herself one," he replied at last, his regard openly mocking.

Dolores smiled disdainfully. "I believe practically every Engishwoman smokes and that the majority wear trouser suits like the men."

Dionis lifted her chin. She was not averse to criticism, but the supercilious remarks of the haughty Dolores irritated like an open wound. "There is nothing new in women wearing trousers," she said quietly. "Eastern women have worn the equivalent for thousands of years and French-women are said to look even more seductive in them." She borrowed Rosalba's impish smile. "I prefer them myself for working in. Not only are they more comfortable, one can bend or climb in them freely without embarrassment."

But Dolores was not to be outdone. "Naturally, when one is doing a man's job," she murmured, "dressing like one is essential."

Here Rosalba came to the rescue and Dionis could have hugged her. "I am sure neither you nor I would look half as attractive in them as Miss Ward does. She is small-boned and very chic in her boyish slimness. My curves, like yours, Dolores, would be rather too obvious."

Dolores pursed her lips primly. "I do not know about you, Rosalba. I would hate to look like a boy."

"I am pleased you are not a boy, Dolores."

Don Juan's eyes twinkled his approval of her feminine charms. No secret here of his admiration for his sister's friend, Dionis thought. His comment partly appeased the Spanish woman, who was now looking round the empty hall. But her target still appeared to be Dionis.

With a look which was openly challenging, she said, "I love this villa and I am sure no improvement could possibly be made on the original furnishings. Would it be presumptuous to ask what exactly you plan to do, Miss Ward?"

Dionis hesitated, hating the idea of disclosing her plans

beneath two pairs of critical eyes. Rosalba was sweet and was no malicious meddler. Dionis liked her and knew she would understand. Dionis had a good knowledge of her work and was confident in her ability to make a success of the job in hand. But it was the thought of wandering through the rooms outlining her plans and drawing nearer to where the wrecked writing table was stored which sickened her. Hoping for the best but expecting the worst, she said, "Not at all. Shall we begin with the kitchen?"

She led the way through the downstairs rooms, outlining her plans as she went. Don Juan asked questions with that quick brain of his always one jump ahead of everything she outlined. Behind her façade of coolness, her thoughts chased each other like demented hornets. However, she did manage to draw the line about going upstairs. Returning to the hall after a tour of the downstairs rooms, Dionis stood and gave brief details of the built-in whitewood furniture she had in mind for the bedrooms and the colourful decorations for each bathroom. When she had finished her face was flushed with the awareness of letting her tongue run away with her. It was something she was apt to do when she warmed up to her favourite subject, her work.

Don Juan said dryly. "Thanks for telling us your plans, Miss Ward. It has been most interesting. As far as I can see there is not much you can do until your materials arrive." He glanced at his wristwatch. "Therefore I suggest you accompany us for a run in the car and return later to the Villa Jacaranda for tea."

To Dionis the invitation after the last gruelling hour was a bit much. Her smile was quite an effort. "I'm sorry. As I feel rather dishevelled I would prefer to return to the inn. Thanks all the same."

"Then you must allow us to offer you a lift." The dark eyebrows lifted in the direction of her floppy-brimmed hat and handbag which she had plonked on the pedestalled rail at the foot of the staircase when she had arrived.

Meekly, Dionis put on the hat and they all walked outside to the long car glittering in the sunshine. Rosalba and

Dolores climbed into the back seat and Dionis was put in front with Don Juan, who slipped in behind the wheel. Paco was hard at work near the gates, his hard-thewn arms stripped to the elbows as he yanked out weeds. Dionis waved and he gave them all a courteous bow. The drive back to the inn was accomplished in silence, with Dionis feeling relegated to the position of being given a lift. She was very conscious of her soiled hands from handling the furniture, her dishevelled appearance and shiny nose against the cool fastidiousness of the two young women behind her. Somehow she felt too worn to care.

She still had not told Don Juan about the writing table. Feeling a far different being from the happy young woman who had set off to work so optimistically that morning, she waited until the car purred to a halt in the courtyard of the inn. Then she was out swiftly, thanking Don Juan for the lift and smiling farewell to his sister and her friend.

That evening Dionis wrote down all the materials she would need for the Villa Acacia and wrote a letter to Angela telling her that Don Juan knew nothing of her fiancé's intention to modernize the villa. She made no mention of the accident to the small writing table – Angela would probably be amused by it. Dionis could imagine her basking on the hot beaches looking fabulous in the briefest of bikinis. To Angela the Villa Acacia was as far away as the moon.

It was a long time before Dionis went to sleep that night. As she tossed and turned in bed she wondered how her former employer, Cesare Delusi, would have reacted to the incident of the wrecked writing table. She could imagine him offering his sincere apologies and replacing it with something equally expensive. She could not do that. She had not that kind of money. Her mouth curved sweetly when she thought of Cesare. What fun he had been to work for, so enthusiastic over every job be it large or small. Congenitally honest and painstaking in his work, he gave of his best unstintingly. His success had been richly deserved and had in no way spoiled him. He sent cheques home to his family in Italy regularly, for he adored his momma and pappa and six brothers and sisters of which he was the eldest. Thinking of Cesare sent her to sleep with a smile on her lips.

After breakfast the next morning Dionis caught the bus to the village. Her errand was mainly to post her letters and to buy stamps. The sooner the list of the materials she needed was sent to London the sooner she would receive them. This morning she was not so downcast. How could she be in the brilliantly warm morning of another perfect day? Her piquant face in the frame of chestnut hair showed a lively interest in everything going on around her. Eagerly scanning the view from the bus window, she glimpsed the narrow winding street of the village shops as the bus rounded a bend to draw up in the little market place. Dionis stepped out to a sleepy silence. Deep awnings and closed jalousies protected shop windows from the heat and dazzle of the sun. Walking past a small gift shop displaying pottery and a garage, she reached the post office and was immediately surrounded by children. They clustered around her, staring at her solemnly with large round dark eyes. Dionis smiled down at them, fondled a black curly head and went into the post office. It amused her to see several of the children sidle into the post office to see what she was buying. She bought stamps and handed over her letters, using her halting Spanish to the postmistress who came to ask her requirements.

The woman was delighted that she spoke Spanish. Her plump face beamed.

"You speak Spanish and understand what I say, and you love children. That I can see."

Dionis laughed, saying her Spanish was very limited. But the woman insisted that she spoke it beautifully. The children smiled their approval and suddenly Dionis found the shop full of customers. The arrival of a young woman from Inglaterra was an event – anything was an event that caused a stir in the charmed air pervading the solitude of a country village. And this young woman was young, vivacious and full of life with dancing eyes and very attractive. They treated Dionis as a friend, asked how long she had been in Spain and if she liked it. Warmed by their friendly reception, Dionis talked with them, slipping in a nod or a smile when she met language difficulties. She bought sweets for the children and left the shop charmed and won over completely by the spontaneous welcome of complete strangers.

In the small gift shop, she lingered and bought mementoes, then wandered down to the spotlessly clean little café where gay tables meandered out on to the pavement. There, Dionis agreed with the proprietor that it was indeed a good morning and ordered coffee and cakes. Savouring each blissful moment of the blue and gold morning, she nibbled a delicious pastry leisurely and drank her coffee. The sun was really hot when she gathered her purchases together to make her way to the bus terminus.

Tercia was inclined to gossip when she waited upon Dionis at lunch time. She had seen her arrive at the inn the previous afternoon in Don Juan's car. So Don Juan had given the *señorita* a lift. What was it like to ride in such an expensive car? Don Juan was so handsome, so exciting. His sister was so beautiful. Tercia did not care for Dolores de Liscondo.

"She has been angling after Don Juan for years." Tercia wrinkled a small nose in a grimace of dislike. "She gives herself airs, that one. I do not believe any of Don Juan's friends would wish him to marry her. The *señorita* is much too self-centred to make him happy."

"She might love him very much," Dionis suggested.

Tercia shrugged. "Not she. She loves his wealth and social position." Setting the last of the dishes on the table, she stood posing gracefully with the empty tray on her hip. Her eyes held a dreamy look. "Always I have longed for a ride in Don Juan's car." She sighed deeply. "I do not think I ever will."

"I don't see why not." Dionis picked up her soup spoon and gave Tercia a fond smile. "One of these days he will

84

be stopping to give you a lift. You will see."

But Tercia shook her head. "*El señor* is so seldom around these parts as a rule. At the moment, he is here to see how the alterations to the inn are progressing. Everyone adores him. When he needs workmen, he has only to lift a finger and the men are there. For *el señor,* they will do anything. For anyone else, they would come and go as they pleased."

When Tercia returned to the kitchen, Dionis discovered that her appetite for the well-prepared lunch was nil. The mention of Don Juan had brought back only too vividly the accident to the small writing table. If he was so prompt at getting things done then he would certainly lose no time in having the furniture removed from the Villa Acacia. He was not the kind of man to leave it in store to deteriorate. She had to see him as soon as possible to explain about the damage to what might well be a family treasure. But how? A letter would take too long. He could act in the meantime. She would have to call and see him personally. The Villa Jacaranda was some distance away, and Spanish women did not go out alone at night, unless accompanied by a duenna. There was this afternoon after the siesta, which left little time before tea.

She was still pondering over how to get there when Tercia returned, aghast to see she had eaten so little.

"Was it not to your taste, *señorita?*" she asked anxiously, removing the practically untouched dishes.

"I'm sorry, Tercia. The lunch as usual is delicious, but I'm not hungry. I think I'm in need of a siesta."

"Are you not well?"

"Yes, of course." Dionis wished she could have confided in Tercia. But it was out of the question. The matter was much too personal. The dark eyes raked her face wonderingly.

"We are going to a *corrida* this evening, *señorita*, a special one for funds to supply the old people with extra food and fuel for the winter. Do you think you will be well enough to come with us? There is a party of us going by bus."

Dionis quelled a sudden shiver. Bullfighting was not in her line and nothing would persuade her to go. Then an idea occurred to her. Watching Tercia fill the tray with the last of the dishes, she asked thoughtfully, "Will it be a private trip? What I mean is, will the coach be calling to pick you up from the inn?"

"*Si, señorita*. The coach will also bring us back to the inn where we shall all have supper. You will come?"

Dionis shook her head. "I'm awfully sorry, I can't go to the bullfight. But I would appreciate a lift as far as the Villa Jacaranda. My fare could go to the proceeds. Could it be arranged?"

If Tercia thought the request a strange one, she did not comment on it. Instead, she replied with all the airiness of youth, "I do not see why not. I will have a word with the driver of the coach. You will be ready to leave at six o'clock this evening."

There were a few elderly women accompanying the two dozen or so young people in the coach when Dionis clambered aboard that evening. Greetings were exchanged and she took the seat nearest the door in order to slip out when she reached her destination. Tercia sat behind her with her *novio*, a likeable young man who strummed a guitar and accompanied it in a good baritone voice. Tercia, a bright peony threaded through her black hair, looked sparkling in a full-skirted dress and open sandals.

Dionis thoroughly enjoyed the ride to the villa; the guitar, the singing amid ripples of laughter brightened an otherwise unenviable journey. She had not the least idea what she was going to say to Don Juan to excuse her carelessness in causing damage to the writing table. Whatever approach she decided upon would disintegrate beneath the steady gaze of a man who was not to be trifled with. On reaching her stop, she alighted and waved the bus out of sight round a bend, realising with deep, heavy heartbeats that the Villa Jacaranda was but five minutes' walk away. She went forward almost with dragging feet, through the elaborately carved gateway leading to the drive. The place lay in a sleepy silence broken by the soft cheep of birds and the slight rustle of feathery palms. Dionis approached the mammoth residence crowned with graceful eaves still and silent amid the shade of trees and exotic plants. There was no sign of life and instinctively she held her breath, fully prepared to walk on tiptoe in case her footsteps would be heard on the gravel path.

She had reached the magnificent courtyard when the sudden sound of voices on the clear evening air sent her swiftly behind the nearest tree. Three figures appeared without warning in the wide entrance porch – Rosalba, Dolores and Don Juan. Dionis stifled a moan of dismay to see his car standing nearby. They were obviously on their way out for the evening. With a pull at her heart-strings, she watched him walk proud and erect with his long easy stride to the car. He looked dangerously attractive in well cut evening dress as quietly and unobtrusively he opened the car door and assisted his two companions inside. Watching him walk round the car to take his place behind the wheel, Dionis knew a wild urge to dash out and stop him before he could set the car in motion. But the idea of explaining her unwarranted intrusion beneath three pairs of startled eyes took more than her kind of courage.

Helplessly, she watched the big car swerve around and sweep along the gravel road until it went from sight. Of course, they could be going to the bullfight if it was for a charitable cause. What bad luck! A few minutes sooner and she might have seen Don Juan before he left. Useless to think of that now. She could not call at the villa and leave a note, for her visit would be sure to raise comment. She could wait for his return and catch him as he was going in. Why not? It was a perfect evening and warm enough to spend outdoors. With her spirits rising from zero Dionis looked around for a suitable spot away from prying eyes at the villa. She found it in a vast old tree branching out into two thick separate trunks a few feet from the ground forming an obliging curve in which she could recline. Sinking gracefully into the hollow, she found it as accommodating as a hammock.

Closing her eyes with the scents of wild thyme, jasmine and wild roses filling her nostrils deliciously, Dionis felt a calmness of spirit washing over her and she slept. She awoke to a sudden chill in all her limbs, feeling the inadequacy of the little woollen white jacket she had unthinkingly slipped on to combat the night chills. Hugging herself for warmth, she sat hunched up, wondering if she had by any chance missed the return of Don Juan to the villa. The Villa Jacaranda still looked silent and deserted with no sign of the car in the courtyard. The rosy glow of early evening had now faded, casting a dark blue curtain over the sky where stars winked at the newly risen moon. Chilled though she was, Dionis allowed her romantic thoughts full rein. What a wonderful place this was for lovers' meeting — a tryst by this beautiful old tree. How many couples had it seen through the years transported to the heights of bliss by the welcoming gleam in each other's eyes?

But such dreams did not keep her warm. She was suddenly aware of chattering teeth and it seemed an age before the arc of a car's headlights lit the sky. As it sped along the road hidden from her view, she prayed that it would not pass the turning to the villa. The sigh of relief she gave when the torchlike beams turned in her direction was audible on the night air. Dazedly and numbed with cold, she watched the long body of the car slide past and whisper to a halt in the courtyard. Don Juan sliding from his seat to open the door for his companions was the cue for Dionis to leave her hiding place. She did so painfully, sure that all her joints were frozen solid. Infusing life into stiff limbs, she fled after him as he followed the two women indoors.

Against the muted lights of the villa, Dionis was like a transparent, graceful ghost. Her hair, a cloudy halo, framed a face in which her long eyes gleamed darkly, anxiously. She seemed scarcely to breathe as she reached out silently to touch his arm. He was startled, to say the least, but he took in the situation and rapidly assumed his usual calm.

As for Dionis, she stood palpitating and breathless, one hand lifted to put a finger against shaking lips, acutely aware of the man confronting her with a narrowing gaze.

She heard his intake of breath. *"Madre mia!"* he exclaimed. "What has happened? Are you in trouble of some kind?" He removed the hand resting restrainingly on his arm to clasp it in his warm ones. "Why, your hand is frozen! Why are you so cold, and what are you doing here all alone? You are alone, are you not?"

Dionis nodded. She was trembling with cold and another strange emotion she was in no fit state to define. "I must talk to you," she whispered urgently. "I won't keep you long."

He led her indoors to a warm, rather austere room of studded leather furniture. There he seated her in a comfortable chair and strode to a cabinet.

"Drink this. It will warm you," he said, returning with a glass of golden liquid. "Take it slowly." He placed the glass in her cold hands, curling her fingers around it with his warm ones.

Her teeth chattered against the glass and she tried to push it away after a few sips. But his hands were around hers like a vice, forcing her to drink every drop. Then, ordering her to stay put, he strode from the room. He was back in minutes with a wine-coloured quilted masculine robe which he helped her into, tucking it around her warmly when she sat down again.

"Now," he said grimly, "you will tell me what has happened." He had perched on the arm of a chair a few feet away from where she sat, his eyes raking her pale face and pinched look. Snug and warm in the dressing robe with the brandy already sending the heat through her body, Dionis was beginning to feel decidedly lightheaded. But her brain remained clear as she told him falteringly about the accident to the small writing table. He listened with set features when she described crawling in beneath the furniture to reach the floor vases.

"I took such care not to disturb anything, and I could

have died when the pile of furniture suddenly swayed and crashed. The leg of the writing-table is beyond repair, I'm afraid. I'm awfully sorry — I would have done anything to prevent it happening." She lifted a face into which the colour was gradually returning. "It's a lovely piece of furniture. I suppose it's valuable."

"It was," he corrected her dryly. "However, I accept the fact that accidents will happen." And suddenly he was leaning forward menacingly, angrily. "What I find so hard to accept are these foolish impulsive actions of yours which are continually landing you into trouble. Namely, clearing the garden seat that day in the heat of the sun, struggling beneath furniture which could have trapped and even maimed you, and now this visit to the Villa Acacia alone and at night."

Dionis stared at him wide-eyed and miserable. "I had to come before you had the furniture removed. Don't you see? I couldn't have had the removal men blamed for something I'd done."

"I doubt if they would have been," he argued uncompromisingly. "Who brought you here tonight?"

There was a short uncomfortable silence, one of those silences holding a warning of unpleasantness to follow. Wondering how she could play down the hours of waiting, Dionis knew with despair that she had to tell him the truth. Winding the silk cord of the dressing gown around her fingers as though to gain courage from it, she told him of her journey there in the coach.

His eyes narrowed shrewdly. "At what time did you have this lift?" he asked quietly.

"A little after six. I arrived to see you leaving in the car, and decided to wait for your return."

He looked incredulous and consulted his watch. *"Dios!* All of five hours. Where did you wait?"

"Sitting in a tree."

"You sat in a tree? I cannot believe it. Why did you not call and leave a message for me?"

Dionis moved uncomfortably, for he was looking at her

as though she had taken leave of her senses. "I ... I thought it might arouse comment."

"And this sitting in a tree like a frightened squirrel — that would not have aroused comment? No?" Don Juan frowned. He looked almost savage. His dark eyes gleamed with a fierce intensity.

"No one saw me. I was well hidden among the trees. I had no idea you would be returning so late," she said in a low voice.

"Late?" he echoed exasperatedly. "Eleven-thirty is not late. The night is only just beginning." Dionis felt his gaze on her bowed head. "What if I had not returned until dawn? You would still have waited?"

She made no answer.

"Well?" he demanded firmly.

He did not raise his voice, but there was something in it that made her quiver. She looked up at him then in swift distress. "No, of course not. If only you knew how terribly sorry I am to have caused you all this upset! And now I'm keeping you from your guest. I must go." She sat up as if to rise, but he stayed her with a restraining hand. Dionis felt choked, unlike herself, curiously passive.

"You must have missed supper," he said, and although his look was grim, his voice was free from harshness. "I will get you something."

His words aroused her as nothing else would have done. "No, please, I beg of you. I couldn't eat a thing. I'm not hungry and have never felt less like eating."

Don Juan had risen to his feet. Pushing his hands into his pockets, he stood regarding her silently, and it seemed to Dionis that neither of them breathed.

At last he spoke slowly and forcefully. "I have a mind to forbid you to continue with this work on the Villa Acacia. What do you say to my giving you a cheque to cover expenses and the time involved? You could spend a holiday here and see everything before going home."

She stared at him aghast. "You mean give it all up when I've already ordered most of the materials? You can't do this to me!"

"Allow me to correct you. I can do as I wish with my own property."

Dionis bit her lip to stop it shaking. His offer had shaken her to the roots. He was right. Wondering how it was all going to end and knowing that this particular job had been doomed from the start, she stared up at him, appalled. With a curious ache in her heart, she realized that in their way of life they were poles apart. Better to have the fact rammed into her now before further complications arose. Sick with disappointment, she freed herself of the robe and stood up, feeling small and defenceless beneath his dark brooding gaze.

"I wonder if you would mind me using your phone to call a taxi from the village?" she asked with a quiet dignity. "I'm sorry I've brought you all this trouble."

He was studying her intently as he would a mathematical problem. To her surprise, when he spoke again his voice was quietly gentle.

"You do not have to apologize for having spent an uncomfortable evening. I will take you back to the inn."

Dionis went with him out to the car. They met no one on the way. All was silent. He helped her into the spacious front seat, tucked a car rug around her warmly and slid in behind the wheel. The car heater was on and she settled back in her seat feeling hollow and spent. Don Juan thrust the long nose of the car forward and soon they were purring along with the headlights lighting up the silent countryside. An owl hooting dismally somewhere above them in the trees found an answering note in her heart. Her visit to the Villa Jacaranda had availed her nothing. Yet she was not sorry. She felt terrible about the wrecked writing table. Somehow it dwarfed all her other problems, this breaking of something valuable that could not be replaced. She would have felt the same in his place, and upon reflection did not blame him in the least for his decision not to allow her to continue at the Villa Acacia. After all, he was not at all happy that his villa should be altered in such a fashion.

Don Juan sat beside her, his profile clear-cut and somehow tight. Dionis tried to assume an air of indifference, found it utterly out of keeping with her sensitive nature and said inpulsively, "I really am sorry about your dear little writing table. I'll do anything to put it right."

"You are living dangerously," he answered without taking his eyes from the road ahead. "That impulsive remark can cover quite a few possibilities." He accelerated and the car beams illuminated trees flanking the road. "Forget it and be thankful it was not your leg that was broken."

"I think I would rather have done that than caused all this trouble," she said ruefully.

"I will not have you wishing harm upon yourself. This thing had to be. However, I shall be happier if you have manual help at hand in future to prevent any further in incidents. You say you have sent for the materials?"

"Yes."

"Immediately they arrive, you are to let me know. I will see that you have assistance. You will require painters, decorators, carpenters and a carpet-laying expert. Am I right?"

"Something like that," she said, her spirits rising as she realized he was going to let her go ahead with her plans. But she had not forgotten Paco's offer of sending along his relations. It was pushing her luck to tell Don Juan this. However, a promise was a promise.

"Paco has relatives in the trade and I more or less promised I would hire them," she said, glancing hopefully at his profile.

"Paco's relatives are no doubt experienced. There is a building boom going on in Spain at the moment and most skilled men are working at full pressure. The men I have in mind are excellent in their work and will stay until the work is finished. I cannot say the same for Paco's relatives, who will probably come when it suits them, a few evenings a week or weekends."

Don Juan spoke with narrowed gaze on the road ahead. It was right what he said, of course. Most skilled men were apt to go after big contracts, fitting in the smaller jobs in between when it suited them. Dionis did not blame them in the least, though it did prove both frustrating and trying when one was given a limited time to finish a job.

"You are very kind," she said warmly. "I fully appreciate your offer and accept it gratefully."

He tossed her a jaded smile. "Do not worry too much about Paco. Some of his relatives are included among the men I shall send to you. In a rural community such as this most of the inhabitants are related to each other." He paused, then said, "I would be pleased if you would accept the loan of one of my cars during your stay. I have several at the Villa Jacaranda, also an excellent driver on whom you can depend. Carlos is out at this moment taking my sister and her guest to call upon friends."

"That is very kind of you, *señor*, and if the Villa Acacia was very far away from the inn, I would accept with pleasure. As it's only a short pleasant walk away I can manage nicely without a car. Thanks all the same."

His voice was decidedly cooler. "I was thinking of tonight. Had you gone to the Villa Jacaranda and asked Carlos to run you back to the inn when I had left he would have done so gladly. He could then have informed me when I returned of your visit and I would have come to the inn at the earliest opportunity to discuss things with you over a glass of wine."

Dionis caught a hint of censure in his voice. He was no doubt regretting the curtailment of a pleasant evening in the company of his sister's friend through her own unexpected appearance.

"Yes, I'm sorry about that. Your guest perhaps will not take kindly to your absence tonight."

He said suavely, "Spanish women are not so independent and usually accept the absence of their hosts or menfolk without question."

She shot him a swift glance. "I find it hard to believe that your women are so lacking in spirit."

"They have spirit. They can love or hate passionately,

94

but they are rather more subtle about their possessiveness."

"An ideal wife from a man's point of view," Dionis murmured. "I'm surprised you've remained a bachelor for so long."

The moment she had spoken she would have given anything to recall her words.

He digested this with extraordinary calm. Indeed, Dionis was beginning to wonder whether he had heard her when he answered in dry cynical tones.

"I am twenty-nine. Do you consider that past the marrying age?"

"Good gracious, no! As a matter of fact I'm of the opinion that no man is mature enough to marry until he's at least twenty-five."

He favoured her with a mocking glance. "Then there is hope for me, would you not say, Miss Ward? Tell me this — at what age would you say a woman was right for marriage?"

"Twenty-one," Dionis answered promptly. "Women usually mature quicker than men."

He said with a hint of satire, "This is all very interesting. Do your powers go as far as giving advice on the kind of partner one should choose?"

Dionis laughed lightheartedly, though she knew no reason why she should feel so happy apart from knowing she could carry on with her job. Her laugh was an enchanting sound, low and husky.

"No. I was only airing my views on the subject," she said demurely.

Something glittered in his dark eyes, a mixture of lively interest and amusement. "How old are you, Miss Ward?"

"Twenty-one."

"Ah, the important age?"

"The age of independence which you so strongly disapprove of in a woman."

"And the ideal age to marry. You have a *novio* in London?"

"A *novio*?" Dionis laughed at her stupidity. "A *fiancé*?

No, I haven't. My work is my only love."

"Speaking of your work," he said, swinging the big car round to enter the courtyard of the inn, "Señora Direnso, a seamstress of some repute who lives in the village, is very clever with her needle. She would only be too delighted to help you with your soft furnishings."

"Why, thanks, *señor*. I'll remember that."

He switched off the engine and turned in his seat to look at her thoughtfully.

"You are warmer now? No shivers after spending your evening in a tree?"

Dionis had to smile. His answering one rocked her heart. "I feel fine, thanks," she answered.

He slid from the car and Dionis had time to unwrap the car rug from round her legs and step out before he came to help her.

"I have asked Señora Lopez to serve you with hot soup and a little refreshment in your room. But first you must take a hot bath to prevent a likely chill." The dark eyes suddenly gleamed maliciously. "You must not risk a chill which might put you back a few days from this work that you love. *Adios*, Miss Ward. Sleep well."

CHAPTER VI

Brushing her hair before her mirror the next morning, Dionis found herself recapping the event of the previous evening with the thought of Don Juan awakening a strange, excited emotion inside her. Something had happened to her during that short journey with his wide shoulder touching her own as the car swerved around hazardous bends. Instinctively, she found herself longing yet dreading the thought of meeting him again. The powerful emotion his presence invariably awoke in her was not love. It was more like a mixture of fear and dismay. There was no doubt that he disapproved of her wholeheartedly. He was only enduring her presence until her job at the Villa Acacia was completed. His suggestion to employ men he could guarantee as being trustworthy had been prompted with the idea of getting the job done in the minimum of time. He was a man who did everything with a purpose — it was to send her packing before she could cause him any more trouble. Besides, she constituted a threat of demoralizing his sister and her woman friend with her ideas of Women's Lib. His sister Rosalba had been reared on graciousness, disciplined by noble gestures and protected from vices by curtailed freedom, and more than likely an arranged marriage was to be her fate. Don Juan would naturally choose a wife like his sister with soft curves, smooth olive cheeks and eloquent dark eyes which would look reproachfully at him when they had words. He, of course, would have the last one. Yet he would make a wonderful lover, Dionis was sure. She had felt the tenderness in his hands when he had tucked the dressing robe about her and again when he had wrapped her in the car rug to take her back to the inn.

Dionis could understand Angela falling for Antonio if he was as attractive as Juan. Well, she would be leaving Spain herself with no complications. And she would never come back. If Angela finally settled in Spain she would be sure to make fleeting visits to London to do her shopping. They would see each other, thus saving Dionis the necessity of going to Spain. Soberly, Dionis went down to breakfast, where Tercia was full of the events of the bullfight the previous evening. Dionis listened, but did not encourage her to talk. The last thing she wanted to hear was a description of the bullfight. The very thought of it made her squirm with pity, not only for the poor wretched bull but also for the unfortunate horses, who though well padded would feel the fiendish thrust of the bull's horns when it constantly charged.

"It was wonderful, and the matador was so handsome and brave," Tercia said enthusiastically. "You must go to see one before you leave, *señorita*. Everyone goes to see a bullfight when they come to Spain."

Dionis smiled and was silent. To Tercia, bullfighting was the national sport, something to be proud of. Dionis shivered. In her opinion the whole thing was barbarous and did not bear thinking about.

She was in her room after breakfast getting ready to go to the Villa Acacia when a knock came on her door. To her surprise she opened it to see Dolores de Liscondo looking as luscious as a peach. The dark eyes and vivid red mouth, however, held a hint of insolence which immediately put Dionis on her mettle.

"*Buenos dias, señorita*. Did you want to see me? Do come in."

Dionis gestured to the one comfortable chair in the room and closed the door.

Dolores entered, declined to sit and rummaged in her handbag to take out a lace-edged handkerchief with the initials D W in one corner. Holding it up by one corner, she dangled it meaningly.

"I found this handkerchief on a chair in Juan's study this morning. I presumed it was yours, since it bears your initials. I saw you using a similar one when we visited you at the Villa Acacia."

98

Aware that this was no friendly visit, Dionis reached out a hand. "Thanks for returning it. I am sorry you made a special journey to return it. It was not that important."

"I did not make a special journey, Miss Ward. Carlos is driving Rosalba and myself to visit friends. I slipped in to return your handkerchief, leaving Rosalba in the car." The lovely eyes hardened. "I saw you last evening getting into Juan's car. I was standing at my window when you left the villa."

Dionis looked at her with no more than a polite interest, although the hot colour crept up beneath her clear skin.

"Really, *señorita*? I had business with Don Juan which does not concern you in the least."

Dolores moved purposefully across the room to lean back against the dressing table to face Dionis. "Anything that concerns Juan concerns me also. You must know we are practically affianced."

Dionis said evenly, "You are both mere acquaintances of mine, therefore I know nothing about your private affairs. Why take the trouble to inform me of them?"

Dolores paled, the small nostrils of her perfect nose distended with hate.

"Because it is essential for you to know that Juan is not as eligible as you appear to believe. He belongs to me."

Dionis looked at the dark smouldering eyes, the set lovely features as Dolores tried to control her emotions, and found she was having to control her own too. The reason for it could only be the Spanish woman's obvious hatred of herself. It had nothing to do with what she had said. Why should it? What did she care if Don Juan was practically engaged to the woman? She spoke with a quiet dignity.

"I still fail to see what it has to do with me."

"Miss Ward." Dolores was now calm and watchful. Her look was one of having underrated her opponent. "You came alone late last evening to see Juan at the Villa Jacaranda. In Spain women of good breeding do not go abroad at night alone, especially to visit a man. Such an action would be totally misconstrued. Juan would not enlighten you about ignoring the proprieties. It is left to you to behave with decorum while you are here."

Dionis controlled her temper with an effort. *"Señorita,"* she said coldly, "your action in coming here using the handkerchief as an excuse to see me leaves me a little confused as to the truth of what you say. If there is an understanding between you and Don Juan then it is not necessary to call to see me at all."

The dark eyes flashed. "I wanted to warn you."

"Warn me?" Dionis echoed, staring at the proud haughty face. "You mean to keep away from Don Juan? Can it be a case of what you cannot have yourself no one else shall?"

Dolores drew herself up indignantly. "How dare you?" she cried.

But Dionis was equal to her anger. "And how dare you come here on such an errand? Too bad you didn't know that your precious Juan doesn't like me nor I him. If you ask him he'll tell you so."

"Why should I ask him? You attach too much importance to yourself, Miss Ward," Dolores said with hauteur.

"On the contrary, you are attaching too much importance to my presence in Spain. You evidently assume that I'm important enough to constitute a threat to your hopes of marrying Don Juan or you wouldn't have come." Dionis, her face pinched and white, moved to the door. "Frankly, *señorita,* I find this conversation extremely distasteful. I would be obliged if you would leave at once."

She opened the door and, to her relief, her visitor swept from the room on a wave of expensive perfume. Closing the door, Dionis walked to the chair and sank into it, conscious of how insidiously the trend of events was pushing her towards greater intimacy with Juan. Had Dolores not come to see her she would have carried on blithely with her job, allowing it to dominate every thought. Now his image was pushing itself back into her mind and from now on she would never be entirely comfortable until they had seen each other for the last time.

Steady on, she told herself. Was this the sensible Dionis Ward, the eager interior decorator with a yen to reach to the top of her profession? – a woman who until now had never been really interested or deeply stirred by any particular man – who had begun to think she never would.

"You have the gift for this kind of work," Cesare Delusi had told her. "You have a flair for colour and design, your ideas are both original and clever and you have the courage to carry them out. There is no reason why you should not reach the top of your profession."

Cesare had seen her as a level-headed, intelligent person, not at all the kind of woman who would fall for a man she had only known for a matter of days. Thank goodness for Cesare! Plenty of time to think of men and marriage when she had proved herself in her work. With the feeling of having reached a milestone in her life, Dionis put the handkerchief away to be laundered, put on her floppy-brimmed hat to keep out the sun and went out to do battle.

She strolled along the white dusty road to the Villa Acacia in her sun suit of blue and primrose, thrilled at the thought of eventually acquiring a tan. All round her the intermittent trillings of birds and the scent of wild flowers in hedges, on bushes and springing from crannies and boulders, filled her with delight. The Villa Acacia slumbered peacefully in the sun and she walked between larkspur, columbine and roses, noting that Paco had done most of the clearing up and was now planting curious little plants which she must remember to ask him the name of. Her visit today was a casual one to open the shutters in all the rooms and let in the sun. The fresh air would penetrate into the floors now that the coverings had been removed and everywhere would be nice and dry for the new décor.

The Villa itself was in an excellent state of repair. There was no smell of damp or condensation when she opened the front door to go up the stairs. Dionis loved the master bedroom with its suite of rooms shut away as it were from the rest of the house. It would be ideal for Angela to spend her honeymoon here. Opening the windows, she went out on to the balcony and looked out across the vineyards and orchards in the distance where the sun glittered on the metal figure of Olympus set high above the garage roof in the village. What fun it would be to have her own car! Too bad she had no permit to drive in Spain. Phew, but it was warm! Taking off her hat, Dionis ran pearl-tipped fingers through her hair where it clung damply to her scalp. Suddenly something on the rim of the stone balustrade caught her eye. A small lizard lay asleep in the sun, its tiny hands outstretched on the hot stone. Smiling gently with delight, she gazed down entranced at the tiny creature who, sensing her presence, opened bright eyes before rapidly disappearing down a crevice in the stone. Still smiling, Dionis found herself peering over to see where it had gone and looked down into the dark eyes of Don Juan, who was standing watching her from below. There was a decided lurch to her heart as their eyes met in a little tingling shock which startled her before it was gone in a flash. His amazing vitality was more dominant than ever in the glitter of his dark eyes as Dionis, wondering how long he had been there watching her, waited for him to speak.

"*Buenos dias*, Miss Ward," he said, his smile white against the deep tan of his face. "The removal men are on their way to collect the furniture."

Dionis gathered scattered wits. "*Buenos dias, señor*," she answered gaily, happiness bubbling inside her strangely. "I'll be right down."

He was standing where she had left him in the sunlit courtyard. Again she was aware of his fitness, born of a strenuous life lived largely in the sun. He turned quickly when he heard her light step to stand looking at her until she joined him. It annoyed her that his intent look could move her so profoundly. There was no sign of his car, which was probably the reason she had not heard him arrive.

Swiftly, he interpreted her look around. "I left my car in a lane nearby in case it should be in the way of the removal van." His tone was deliberately casual. "May one ask what it was you were looking at so intently just now on the balcony?" His mouth curved into a smile, seeing again the sun on her chestnut hair, the red lips so sweetly curved and the tender look in the long hazel eyes.

To her annoyance, she blushed. "I was watching a tiny lizard. Unfortunately it disappeared before I could make its acquaintance."

He raised a dark brow in that very attractive way he had. "You were not afraid of it?"

"Goodness, no. It was very sweet." She had to look away then from the glittering intent gaze before she could go on. "The two floor vases I mentioned last evening – could I borrow them? They would go very well with the kind of lounge I have in mind. It would be better than keeping them in store." Dionis bit her lip, hoping he would not think it cheek on her part to mention them after wrecking the writing table.

"Have them by all means," was the answer, and she was relieved to see he was still smiling. "I suggest we return to the balcony where you saw the small lizard to watch the men loading the furniture. Then, if you see anything else you fancy, just say the word and I will instruct them to leave it behind."

"You mean that, *señor*?" she asked, wide-eyed.

"I seldom say anything I do not mean."

They were smiling at each other when the removal men arrived, and while he had a word with them, Dionis made her way up to the balcony. Suddenly the villa was an enchanted place with all her antagonism against him gone as though it had never been. She was looking down into the crevice where the tiny lizard had disappeared when he joined her. Silently, he looked down at her sudden confusion and hesitant smile and his own smile was infinitely charming.

Dionis was glad of the removal men taking his attention, for she felt a sudden unaccountable shyness as she stood beside him with his wide shoulder so near. The men had now emptied the van of packing and were now mounting the stairs to bring down the furniture. Nervously, she waited for the wrecked writing table to appear, knowing how embarrassed she would be when it did. When it was not among the first half dozen articles to be brought out, Dionis could only think it had been put to one side to be sent away later for repair. When one of the three removal men carried out a carved ebony pedestal, Don Juan slanted her a glance. "What about that? I believe pedestals are often used in modern décor to good effect?" he asked with a twinkle.

"Yes, please. It will look charming."

"With the chest?" he finished for her, noticing her eyes on a beautifully matching chest the other two removal men were taking to the van.

"May I?" she asked delightedly.

Dionis saw him give the man a signal with mixed feelings. This was something she had never expected in her wildest dreams, Don Juan not only allowing the modern décor but taking a hand in it too.

"I know a little bit about modern décor," he said, catching her surprised glance. "The last exhibition in Madrid drew large crowds. I went myself. I am not saying I prefer it or even condone it. To me this modern trend is entirely without charm or character." He gave an alien shrug. "I admit that some of it is brilliantly designed and sculptured, but none of it has any soul. I prefer the graceful charm of elegant furniture and buildings created by men dedicated to their job. I remember as a boy experiencing a warm feeling of security in the solid background of my home, as if my ancestors were still around giving me an example of something to look up to and be proud of."

Dionis, warmed by his sudden confidence, said impulsively, "You've been to London, *señor*?"

"Quite often. I go on business. I also took a course in Ancient History at Cambridge. Why?"

"Because it's the place I love best in all the world, and probably for the same reason that you prefer your ancestral home. To me every brick and stone of the old London still lives and breathes." Dionis went on to talk about the dear old Abbey, grey and worn, venerable with age, peopled with ghosts from a glorious past and hallowed by deeds of service. "There's no place in the world so soul-stirring, so inspiring as Westminster Abbey for making one feel proud and humble, for giving one an anchor and a reason for being. I understand your sentiments, *señor*, and respect them."

"I believe you do." There was a strange look in his eyes. "I, too, experienced that feeling when I walked in its dimness. Cambridge and Oxford are two other such places. None of the soulless modern, box-like buildings built by progress could ever instil that wonderful urge to live up to past glories and to rise above them as the old gracious buildings do."

Dionis laughed softly, happily, an enchanting tinkle of amusement.

"Nothing personal," she said hurriedly at his raised brows. "Like all men, you want to go one better and rise above former deeds of valour."

He became at once teasing and vital. "Why not? It's the natural masculine reaction to deeds of glory. My ancestors, like yours, Miss Ward, were conquerors." He gestured down towards the removal van. She nodded and the beautiful Chinese screen the men had brought down was put aside at his signal.

Paco was working in the garden when they went downstairs after the removal men had gone. Juan enquired about his knee, congratulated him on his work of setting the garden to rights and suggested several orange trees in tubs to replace the old dilapidated ones in the courtyard. Then, because he appeared to expect it, Dionis walked with him to his car. He smiled down at her as they walked the few paces down the lane to where his car was parked.

He opened the door of the car. "I have the pleasure of taking my sister and her friend to Barcelona for the day tomorrow by car. They are eager to see the bullfight in the afternoon when a famous matador will be the star performer. Have you been to a bullfight, Miss Ward?"

Dionis shivered inwardly. "No."

"Then why not come with us?"

Frantically, Dionis searched for a feasible excuse, mindful of his kindness and for the fact that he was anxious for her to see the national sport.

"I'm sorry, I'm not a ... an *aficionada*." She felt her face grow hot. "I think that's the word for a bullfighting fan."

"It is." He sounded mildly surprised. "You are not curious to see a bullfight before you leave Spain?"

"I should hate to see an animal killed, *señor*."

"I admire your sentiments, but are you not just a little curious to see the ring? You need not stay for the actual performance. The grand overture when a notable star is taking part is quite impressive. Also you will find much that will interest you in Barcelona. The shops in the Paseo de Garcia would delight you."

Dionis hesitated, not wishing to offend. After all, she was thinking of going to Barcelona to purchase a few materials to carry on with her work at the Villa Acacia before the bulk of her order arrived from London. But a bullfight? Never!

He waited for her answer, his hand on the door of his car. "Perhaps you will think it over and let me know," he said, his eyes on her uncovered head. "Meanwhile I have your promise to always seek Paco's assistance in tasks requiring masculine skill?"

"Yes."

"And I will await your decision about tomorrow."

His tone was negligent, his manner easy enough to enable her to extricate herself without embarrassment. She took advantage of it.

"I have already decided, *señor*. I'm sorry, but thanks for asking me."

He bowed his dark head, making no attempt to persuade her to change her mind. Dionis knew a swift moment of regret as he slid in his car, lifted his hand in a farewell gesture and drove away. Too bad he happened to be going to

Barcelona on the day she planned to go. It certainly would not prevent her from going. She would be going by bus. There was no reason why their paths should cross.

CHAPTER VII

THAT afternoon after her siesta Dionis, in sun suit, shady hat and sunglasses, went for a walk. There was nothing more to do at the Villa Acacia until her materials arrived. Some of the smaller items she intended to order from Barcelona when she went the next day. Without any set idea as to where she was going she walked leisurely along admiring the views. It occurred to her as she made her way along the white dusty road that the three predominant colours in Spain were black, white and red.

Black for the wearing apparel, white for the villas and cottages, and red for the tropical flowers. There had been heavy showers of rain during the night, but the day's heat had dried away all sign of it. All day the sky had persisted in its blueness and everything, trees, vineyards, orchards against a backcloth of distant hills, stood out starkly in the brilliant light. In the blue distance on a hill, she could see a goatherd sitting back against a rock, his head nodding forward in sleep. When several donkeys, heavily panniered, ambled by with their owners, she smiled warmly with a courteous greeting. It was returned with equal warmth. The car came from nowhere to slide silently to a halt beside her. Only Don Juan could drive so expertly, she thought, preparing to meet the dark eyes with a hastily assumed calm she was far from feeling. She felt him take in the pretty sun suit patterned with white daisies on a blue ground, the sunglasses and the wide-brimmed white hat underlined in blue, appraising her cool, poised look.

Leaning sideways, he flicked open the door of the car. "*Buenas tardes*, Miss Ward. Not walking to Tarragona, by any chance?"

She smiled, annoyed at the heavy drumming of her heart against her ribs. "Not exactly. I fancy it would be a bit too far. I'm enjoying a walk in your wonderful unpolluted air."

"As it happens I am on my way to Tarragona on business which will not keep me long. Would you care to accompany me? We could have tea and you would see a little of a really fascinating city." He lifted a tantalizing brow.

"I'd love to. Thank you very much." Dionis slipped in beside him, every detail of his appearance stamped indelibly on her memory for all time.

He was wearing white slacks with a matching silk shirt opened at the neck to accommodate a crimson silk scarf. His excellently tailored black jacket was monogrammed on the breast pocket and he wore it with an air. Again the black, white and red, she mused, his charming appearance bringing a curious ache to her heart.

Relaxing against the expensive leather upholstery, Dionis watched the passing scenery as they purred along pleasurably.

"How are you liking it here in Spain?" he asked casually.

"I'm loving it. I love everything about it, especially the sun."

He shot her a brief glance. "You are not weighted down by tradition or irritated by our casual way of living at all?"

"I do find it strange, but it's an essential part of the charm."

"How long are you staying, Miss Ward? Until the job is done?"

"I suppose so. I'm aching to get started. I hate this hanging about."

"But you will find time to relax after working hours to enjoy yourself?"

He slowed down to go gently round a donkey carrying a man in a large panama hat.

"Oh yes!" Dionis gave him an impish smile because she felt so lighthearted. "During the siesta."

"One feels you have the hankering to despise our siesta. A Spanish husband would insist upon it." He gave her a speculative glance. "Could you imagine yourself married to a Spaniard?"

"No, I could not," she volunteered firmly.

He raised a brow mockingly. "So emphatic? Yet you have a sister who is affianced to one. You're afraid?"

Dionis did not answer immediately. She was visualizing a siesta spent with him and was shattered by emotions both obscure and disturbing. She wanted to speak of Dolores, but they were not friendly enough to discuss his private affairs.

"Not afraid," she said at last. "Merely cautious."

"You would have me believe you are cautious in love when you are so impulsive by nature. Could it be that you have an unfortunate experience in love to make you cautious?" He looked for a swift second into her clear eyes, then gave his attention once more to the road. "No, that cannot be it, for you have an innocent, unawakened look."

"Innocent or naïve?"

He laughed. "You have the Spanish temperament already! This quickness to take offence. You blush so easily at the least embarrassment, and also," again the mocking look, "at your own thoughts."

"*Señor!*" she cried, half in dismay. Her colour deepened. Heaven forbid that he could read her thoughts!

Suddenly he threw back his head to roar with laughter. After that, everything was easy between them. Juan pointed out places of interest, adding historical details, and she listened, enthralled by his knowledge of his country. When they came to a rise in the road, she found herself looking in the distance to the city of Tarragona. She sat up delightedly.

"It's like something out of the Middle Ages, a study in sepia like an old valuable print," she cried.

He agreed. "In Roman times, Tarragona was an important stronghold. Unfortunately the cathedral is rather crammed in between other buildings, but it is well worth a visit. There is also a monastery about twenty-five miles from the city at Poblet which I would like to take you to see some time. It was built in the twelfth century. The improvements added to it through the years make it one of the most remarkable monasteries in Spain."

They were on the outskirts of the city when he said, "I am dropping you off at a hotel before we enter the town. The idea is for you to enjoy a cool drink while I conduct my business. Then I will return to pick you up."

He turned the car off the road to take a side upward gradient. There were glimpses of a white building between palms and cedars and Dionis heard the sound of running water. Then they were sliding to a halt outside the grand entrance to a hotel, an impressive domed building surrounded by trees and feathery fronds outlined clear and sharp against a vivid blue sky. Don Juan piloted Dionis up the steps and a uniformed porter wearing white gloves swung open the door with an expansive smile. In the reception lounge, Dionis was seated by a window with a panoramic view of the town and the coastline. Juan gave rapid instructions to a waiter, lifted a hand and was gone.

"*El señor* said an iced sherry for the *señorita*," the waiter said, placing a glass of sparkling wine before her with the cool tinkle of ice in its depths.

Dionis thanked him, raised the drink to her lips and found it cool and refreshing. At the far end of the lounge she could see the entrance to a cocktail bar, a long black-tiled room with overhanging bronze lamps echoing the gold of rich furnishings against the black walls. Cool and dim inside, it was occupied by about half a dozen men. Dionis smiled. Was that the reason Juan had put her in the lounge? She was apt to forget that women in Spain were usually chaperoned. Yet despite the courtesy, the old traditions, one could sense a brooding passion beneath the surface, a simmering violence in a country of contrasts. It was there in the beautiful savagery of brilliant exotic blooms which spilled over defiantly, uncontrollably from terraces and stone walls like tempers could do.

Dionis marvelled at the calm acceptance of arranged marriages with so much effervescent spirit and emotion simmering beneath the surface. Don Juan would accept it. He was too well disciplined to allow his heart to rule his head. Her thoughts drifted to Dolores and she began to feel strangely hollow inside. Was she envying the women?

"Another drink, *señorita*?"

The waiter was again at her side as she emptied her glass.

"I think not, *gracias*. I will wait for *el señor*."

"As you wish, *señorita*. The powder room is to the left at the foot of the staircase."

She was seated again where he had left her when he entered the room. Several female heads turned in his direction as he strode across to her. And again it struck her how very attractive he was, so intensely alive with his vitality fusing itself into an outward expression of abundant energy as he reached her with a brilliant smile.

"Did you enjoy your drink, Miss Ward?" he asked politely.

"Very much, thank you, *señor*. It was most refreshing."

"*Bien*. Shall we go?"

He smiled down at her as she rose to her feet and she was very conscious of his hand on her arm as they walked to his car.

Dionis found the walled-in city of Tarragona enchanting. They went through the cathedral and lingered around the shops where Dionis made several purchases of small gifts for friends. Her warm personality and friendly smile captured the hearts of the courteous shopkeepers who were always so eager to please. She chuckled deliciously over her stumbling mistakes in Spanish and her eyes danced. Sometimes Juan murmured a word here and there to help her, and although she blushed with embarrassment when she met his eyes, she had to laugh.

There was a poignant moment in a little bookshop when Juan placed a book in her hand.

Curiously, she looked at the spine. "*Platero y Yo*, by Juan Ramón Jimenez," she read aloud, and looked up at him wonderingly.

"I have seen you gazing tenderly on our soft-eyed donkeys," he said, his eyes on her face. "I want you to accept this little book as a memento of this day. It is the life story of a small donkey named Platero. I hope you like it."

Dionis shone up at him her long eyes alight with pleasure. "Like it?" she echoed. "I shall love it. Thank you very much, *señor*. It is indeed kind of you." She looked extraordinarily young and vividly alive, clasping the book as if it was some valuable prize. Then catching her breath on a bubble of laughter, she said impishly, "It's certainly an incentive to learn your language. Are you appalled at my use of it?"

"On the contrary, I found it very entertaining and refreshing." His smile held a touch of the old mockery. "And now I am sure you are more than ready for refreshment. I suggest we call back at the hotel for tea."

They walked back to his car with Dionis amazed at how the time had flown. Arriving at the hotel, they had tea on the terrace. They sat in white cane chairs softened by gay cushions and a waiter brought them tea and cakes. The other tables were occupied by the usual crowd of smart cosmopolitans one usually met abroad in the smart places. Someone at the far end of the terrace was strumming a guitar and presently broke out into a flamenco song. It was a strange sad air, infinitely tragic, filling the air with foreboding. So it seemed to Dionis, who sensed a change in the atmosphere between herself and Juan. The intimacy of the last two hours had gone, with Juan presenting her with an enigmatic profile. He had refused the small pastries, had asked her permission to smoke and was now enjoying a cheroot as he gazed out into the distance, deep in thought.

Dionis nibbled a pastry with an absurd desire to run her fingers through his black springy hair, anything to bring his thoughts back to her presence.

"Have you completed your business?" she asked for want of something to say.

Casually, he blew out a line of smoke before giving her his attention.

"I have. Later this evening I am giving a small business dinner at the Villa Jacaranda, then I shall be free tomorrow." He paused and she saw the faint query in his eyes.

"You have not changed your mind about going with us to Barcelona tomorrow?"

Dionis shook her head. Already she was feeling guilty at having spent the afternoon with him. There was nothing to be gained by a friendship with Don Juan Vicente de Velez y Stebelo, however casual. And that was all it ever could be. They belonged to different worlds. Perhaps he felt the same, for he said no more. Later, when he returned her to the inn, the firecracker spraying her day with happiness had fizzled away like a damp squib.

Dionis caught the coach to Barcelona the next morning convinced that a complete break away from her problems was what she needed. A day in the city among gay crowds would do much to banish disturbing thoughts. She had endured a surfeit of them since arriving in Spain. With this thought in mind she had packed her swim suit and towel in a beach bag along with whatever else she would require for her day out and settled down in her seat on the coach to gaze out on familiar country. After a while, the scenery was not so interesting and there was a spell of passing through rather desolate landscape before they reached the outskirts of Barcelona.

Again it was a bright sunny day, enlivening the usual suburbs of a city with its colourful gardens and white villas shuttered and silent in the heat. Soon they were cruising down a wide boulevard of smart cafés and restaurants to the Plaza de Cataluna. The coach pulled in behind a fleet of double-decker buses and Dionis alighted at the terminus. She found herself in a large square where a fountain, flower beds, trees and statues formed a centrepiece surrounded by buses and trams. Outdoor cafés, office blocks and flats formed a modern backcloth and Dionis responded immediately to the easy-going charm, almost tangible beneath the quickened tempo of city life. Roads radiated from the huge terminus with the tree-lined Paseo de Garcia heading to the west and the obscurity of distant hills and plains. To the east were the Ramblas, a long tree-shaded walk cutting through the faded elegance of the old part of the town.

With the object of buying materials for the small jobs at the Villa Acacia, Dionis lost no time in catching a bus to the shops. She was fortunate to be able to purchase the things she wanted and, after an assurance of an early delivery from obliging assistants, she felt free to enjoy her day. By this time the shops were closing for lunch and the afternoon siesta and the news stands were doing a brisk trade with last-minute shoppers. Ignoring the posters advertising the bullfight that afternoon, Dionis made a beeline for the beach. Soon she was in a more humble part of the town where tall buildings hemmed in narrow streets of cafés, restaurants and bars frequented by seamen. She came upon the charming little fishing village quite unexpectedly at the end of a steep narrow winding street. Delighted, she gazed upon humble whitewashed dwellings with red roofs and blue shutters in a small secluded bay. In the far corner a formation of overhanging rocks formed a shallow cave offering shelter from the sun and privacy. The beach was deserted and she made her way happily to the shade of the rocks.

The next half hour swimming in the warm sparkling water was sheer bliss. No one had appeared to disturb her privacy when she trod along the warm sand to sink down contentedly on her towel. The packed lunch given to her by Señora Lopez was enough for three people. Dionis ate leisurely, wrapped in a cocoon of warmth and a silence broken only by the gentle lap of the waves on the shore. Nothing stirred beneath the canopy of blue sky except two ships moving slowly across the horizon. The thought occurred of how easy it would be to drift into a lotus-eating existence where cool shuttered rooms beckoned and where energetic movement was confined to long leisurely nights dining with friends. One needed the iron restraint of Don Juan to defy the heat. It did not bother him. He strode through it as he had strode into her life, virile, disturbing and wholly masculine. Her heart ached at the thought of him somewhere perhaps quite near with Dolores.

Dionis bit into the ripe black olive, refusing to recognise

the sudden sweep of emotion as jealousy. But it was — a swift thrust of painful emotion which she instantly banished as being too ridiculous for words. It made no sense to someone like herself who was not given to swooning over men. All the same, the thought of him left her not only breathless but stimulated and gloriously alive. But not for her the premonitory pain of unrequited love. Better to dismiss him from her thoughts before he had too big a hold on them. The satisfying lunch and the soft lull of the sea in the warm air made her drowsy. The soft warm sand was as comfortable as a bed and her eyes closed as she snuggled down in it.

Dionis awoke to the sound of whisperings and soft suppressed giggles. Opening her eyes, she saw four small children regarding her solemnly with great black eyes. They were neatly but very poorly clad and were dark, dimpled and delicious. Dionis thought immediately of grapes and peaches and hot sun of which they were the babes. As she sat up their laughter bubbled forth tinkling like hidden mountain springs and they backed away. Dionis hugged her knees.

"*Buenas tardes, niños,*" she said, looking on them fondly, warmly.

"*Buenas tardes, señorita,*" they replied in chorus, moving nearer as they became bolder.

"*Vuestros nombres, por favor,*" she said, leaning forward for their reply.

"Maria, Carmen, Paquita and José," they answered in turn, each accompanying their name with a little courteous bob.

Dionis chuckled, her heart going out to the small José with his shy smile and tangle of rough black curls. She reached for the remains of the generous lunch, omelette sandwiches, cold meats and fruits, and painstakingly divided them into four equal portions.

They set upon it joyously. Soon every crumb was eaten and she pressed pesetas into each grubby little hand for them to go and buy ice cream. Scurrying away, they turned before leaving the beach to wave farewell. She waved back, consulted her watch and discovered she had slept right through the siesta. Another bathe in the warm sea and she would make her way back to the town.

The tram she boarded was filled with people obviously fresh from their siesta on the way to the bullfight, for they talked volubly of the Plaza de Toros. It was morbid curiosity which prompted her to join the crowd on leaving the tram and make her way towards the Plaza de Toros. The hot pavement burned through her sandals as she walked past vendors of peanuts, drinks and souvenirs. Then, with a jolt of her heart, she was staring at the round arena. The hot air vibrated with alien cries as she stood near the entrance watching people queueing up to enter.

Numbly, she saw them purchase a leather cushion with their ticket of admission to soften the hard impact of the stone seats around the arena. She shuddered. The great round building was symbolic of an alien cruelty and the sudden loud bellowing of young bulls in their corral, unaware of the fate that awaited them, proved too much for her. Dionis moved away on a wave of revulsion, away from the threat of blood and sweat which would be the order of the day from the triumphal entry of the spectacular procession into the bullring to the final killing of the poor wretched bull.

Gradually, the horror was forgotten when she strolled along the central walk of the Ramblas, where sunshine filtered through the plane trees, throwing lacy patterns at her feet. It fell on the faded elegance of Spanish architecture and on the bright tiers of banked flowers displayed by vendors lining the route. Dionis enjoyed walking around the gift shops where souvenirs of Spanish workmanship were relatively cheap. The leather work was of the highest quality. She bought gifts for friends and a soft cream leather handbag for Angela, neat, capacious and superbly finished. Her stroll along the tree-shaded walks was made interesting by the poise and graceful carriage of the Spanish women who were exquisitely dressed and well groomed. She also noticed the fastidious appearance of the men, whose footwear was polished to perfection by the *limpiabotas* or shoeblacks who abounded in the city. Later, she visited the large market, by-passing the meat stalls displaying a gruesome selection of every part of a slaughtered animal's anatomy and was fascinated by the fierce, almost human faces of some of the Mediterranean fish on display.

Small side roads in the Ramblas sheltered fascinating taverns, immaculate and very inviting with their raftered ceilings and brass lamps gleaming softly in shade. Her last dip in the sea had sharpened her appetite and Dionis could not resist the menu they offered. So, sitting at a small immaculately clean table in the tavern of her choice, she ordered the speciality of the day – an old Spanish dish called *zarzuela*. A fish stew, it consisted of lobster, prawns, mussels and other shellfish and was well known for being nourishing and sustaining. It was delicious. At last, replete and just a little guilty at spurning the usual light tea, Dionis set off for the bus terminus.

"Miss Ward? What are you doing here?"

The deep familiar voice caused her heart to move and flutter like a wild bird. Soft pink lips slightly parted, she gazed up into the dark eyes of Don Juan, who was staring down at her incredulously.

"Combining business with pleasure." She smiled because she felt so happy, saw his mouth thin and hastened on, "I came to order materials for the Villa Acacia and have spent the rest of the day sightseeing."

He frowned broodingly. "Are you alone?"

"Yes," she said blithely. "I'm on my way to the bus terminus."

Dionis saw the slight tautening of his jaw. "The bus? When you might have travelled by car at my invitation?" He allowed himself a leisurely glance at the salt bloom on her cheeks, the beach suit, beach bag, bulging handbag and several gay parcels in her arms. "But why, when you knew I was coming to Barcelona?"

Treating the distinct chill in his manner lightly, Dionis

smiled up at him.

"You were going to the bullfight, *señor*, and I didn't wish to inconvenience you in any way. You might have felt obliged to forgo your pleasure and take me round the city. One way or another, I've inconvenienced you far too much already."

Don Juan was as cold as a glacier. He made an impatient gesture with a lean brown hand. "You are much too independent, Miss Ward. I do not care for you to behave in such a manner. As a visitor to this country it is to your benefit that you accept any offer to make your stay here as pleasant as possible. You will return to the inn by car. I insist."

"But . . ." Dionis began to protest, only too aware of her appearance. She felt and looked like a day tripper, and would be compared unfavourably with his smart sister and the haughty Dolores. But there was nothing else for it. He was already taking her parcels and the beach bag before marching her to where his car was parked. She was put in the spacious front seat with her belongings beside her and he slid behind the wheel. As they sped towards the new part of the town, Dionis gazed miserably through her window, bewailing the fact that another quarter of an hour would have seen her on the bus making her own way back to the inn. Where Rosalba and Dolores were, she had no idea. It was sufficient to know that he was going to pick them up.

In no time at all they were cruising along wide modern roads. Traffic moved smoothly in a highly organized fashion with no one abusing the highway code by jockeying for the lead. Presently he turned the car off the road into the car park of a rather grand hotel. He helped her from the car and she stared up at a terrace running the whole length of the hotel. Between arched portals waiters were moving between tables supplying guests with tea.

Don Juan was immediately recognised by one of the waiters who came forward to greet him courteously with a deferential air.

"You will please to come this way, *señor*. I trust the table is to your liking."

He led them along the beautifully tiled terrace to a table strategically placed to give a view between marble pillars supporting Moorish archways. There was a panoramic view of the immaculate grounds which included the wide sweep of marble steps leading up to the grand entrance.

Don Juan smiled charmingly, approvingly. "*Gracias,* Luis. It will be tea for four, *por favor*."

Luis went to carry out the order while Juan seated Dionis at the table, taking his seat opposite to her with consummate ease. Dionis was about to tell him she had already had tea when she saw him looking towards the entrance of the hotel. Following his gaze, she saw Rosalba and Dolores walking up the steps and along the terrace to their table.

"We have put our purchases in the boot of the car, Juan," Rosalba said as he seated her. Then she was looking at Dionis in pleased surprise. "Miss Ward! How nice to see you." She sat in a poise of incomparable grace, not a hair out of place, soignée and cool in a beautifully tailored dress of black taffeta and lace.

Juan had seated Dolores, and Dionis had not missed the dark burning glance in her direction. The hauteur of her expression, the sudden pouting of the red lips told of her dislike for the woman from Inglaterra. Her brief nod was one of superb arrogance. But the smile she turned on Don Juan was singularly sweet.

"You did not tell us that Miss Ward was to take tea with us, Juan." The black level brows lifted at Rosalba. "Did you know, Rosalba?"

Don Juan cut in smoothly before his sister could reply, "Miss Ward is in Barcelona for the day. She will be returning with us in the car."

The black brows went up still further. "Did you not come by car, Miss Ward?" Dolores fixed her with a cool stare.

"I came by bus."

120

Dolores curled her red lips. She could not have looked more surprised had Dionis admitted to travelling to Barcelona in a cattle truck.

"You are accustomed to travel by bus, Miss Ward. You have no car?"

Dionis said firmly, "No, not at the moment. I'm hoping to acquire one when I return to London. It's essential to my work."

"Ah, yes – your work. You English women are truly remarkable. You are happy to ride in buses and rub shoulders with *gitanas*. Then you return home to run your own business." Again the brilliant smile on Juan. "Can you imagine Rosalba or me doing these things, Juan?"

He said dryly, "Miss Ward possesses an adventurous spirit. Doing the unconventional emphasizes her independence."

Dolores gave Dionis a spiteful glance. "Would you not agree, Juan, that Miss Ward could benefit from her visit to Spain?"

Don Juan's expression was enigmatic, but Dionis had the idea of him speaking with his tongue in his cheek. "On the contrary, we stand to benefit considerably by her visit to us. She is apparently much talented, exceedingly clever and artistic."

Dolores had an expression of scarcely veiled triumph. "Juan is not being very complimentary to you, Miss Ward. No Spaniard would ever tell one of his countrywomen that she was clever or talented. The correct compliment, and one that every Spanish woman expects as her right, would be to tell her she is beautiful." Her smile was knife-edged. "No doubt you are also unaware that Spanish women are encouraged to grow up beautiful, with their femininity encouraged by the use of all the womanly arts which make them so. The boys grow up learning to increase their masculinity by deeds of physical daring and courage. Here in Spain there is no difficulty in recognising the sexes."

"But, Dolores," Rosalba remonstrated, "no one could dispute Miss Ward's sex. She is so utterly feminine and very pretty. I envy her English rose complexion. I am sure she will have great difficulty in repulsing admirers during her visit."

The arrival of a waiter with a loaded tray put an end to further conversation. In addition to the tea and tiny pastries, he placed three silver dishes of wild strawberries and cream before the three women. Dionis looked down at her portion with misgiving. Since eating the more than satisfying seafood at the tavern her appetite was nil. Now was the time to say she had already eaten, but something glittering in the dark eyes of Dolores kept her silent. She did, however, refuse the small pastries Rosalba offered.

"No pastries, Miss Ward? Do not tell me you are slimming, with that lovely slender figure." She smiled cajolingly, showing small pearly teeth. "Try one with your strawberries and cream. They are delicious eaten that way."

"Are you not partial to strawberries and cream? You have them in England, I believe. Juan knows Rosalba and I cannot resist them, and he naturally assumed that you cannot either." Dolores flashed him a provocative look. "It is my belief that your guest ate too many titbits at the bullfight this afternoon. The trays of refreshments were tempting and I noticed many of the English present appeared to never stop eating."

"I am afraid I, like many more of my own people, could not stomach your bullfighting, *señorita*. As for the refreshments, most visitors of any nationality would enjoy the unique experience of sampling them," Dionis said politely.

Rosalba poured out tea. Juan accepted his laced with lemon to say suavely, "Miss Ward does not care for our national sport, Dolores. I gather it was the reason she refused to come with us today."

Rosalba gave Dionis a warm smile. "I am sure you would have enjoyed it. It is all so thrilling and exciting. The matador was so handsome and brave."

Don Juan regarded Dionis steadily across the table. "My sister means that a first-class bullfight can be both novel and entertaining. The pomp and pageantry is most impressive, and a first-class matador is well worth seeing. He has his performance worked out to a fine art. He reaches perfection via three important channels. The first is known as style or *parer*. To attain this he has to remain impassive when the bull charges. By sheer skill and grace of movement he compels the animal to give way and go round him instead of vice versa. The second skill is known as *mander*, a complete mastery over the bull, every movement calculated to reduce it to wax in his hands. The third is timing or *templar*. Every movement must appear leisurely and completely without fear, never hurried. It is like a banquet where every drop of wine, every tantalizing crumb of food is savoured to the last morsel. That is why only a Spaniard can become a first-class bullfighter. Only he has the gift of refusing to be hurried, thus giving the maximum of entertainment."

Dionis had forced herself to listen. To a Spaniard it was no doubt the acme of entertainment. In her opinion the whole thing was bestial and deplorable.

"Yet for all their leisureliness, your countrymen can be capable of violence and passion. I find that rather confusing," she said quietly.

The dark eyebrows rose mockingly and her heart rocked. "Could be the Moorish strain revealing itself in times of stress or deep emotion. Passion is all the more intense when it is allowed to smoulder."

"As I said, Juan." Dolores, tucking into her strawberries and cream, was reinforcing herself for battle. The lovely shoulders lifted. "Miss Ward would never understand our nature. We are of different worlds."

Dionis, eyes lowered to her dish, was aware of Juan changing the subject with a smoothness indicative of his thoughts well away from bullfighting. Beneath his guidance conversation flowed easily with Dionis completely captivated by Rosalba's charm and friendliness. Like her brother, she had the same nonchalant way of listening with a definite twinkle in her lovely dark eyes, so enchanting in her, so disturbing and exciting in Juan. Dionis knew that the impression he made upon her became more vivid with each encounter. So it was hardly surprising to find her stomach behaving strangely before she ate the strawberries and cream. None of the women smoked after their meal and it was left to Juan to give the signal for them to leave when he had finished his cigar.

Dionis was not sorry when they made a move for his car. Despite Rosalba's warm friendliness, she had a feeling of butting in where she was not wanted. Dolores had clearly indicated it, and her presence had not allowed Dionis to forget it. The silence which fell between them when they were all seated in the big car was a welcome one, although Dionis would have preferred not to have shared the front seat with Juan.

Since her arrival in Spain, she had been fairly cautious about eating the strange food. She had eaten sensibly with the knowledge that most Spanish dishes were cooked invariably in oil and, as such were a challenge to the strongest of English stomachs. How unwise she had been to eat the strawberries and cream so soon after the substantial meal at the tavern was soon evident by the peculiar way her stomach began to behave as their journey got under way. Several severe pains darted across her stomach with mercurial swiftness. Oh, goodness, she hoped she was not going to be ill before they reached the inn. Juan was driving at speed, and for the first time since her arrival in Spain, the scenery meant nothing to her. Rosalba and Dolores were talking quietly in the back of the car and she was thankful that they did not include her in their conversation. She could not have answered them rationally. The agonizing pains in her stomach were coming too frequently for that. Feverishly her eyes sought a landmark through the windscreen that would tell her they were nearing the inn, but Don Juan appeared to be taking roads she did not recognize.

Her tenseness could have alerted him to her condition, for he turned his head with a smothered exclamation at the sight of her ashen face as she lay with her head back against the upholstery. There was the sudden movement of hastily applied brakes and he pulled in at the side of the road.

"What is it, Miss Ward? Do you not feel well?" He placed the back of his hand against her forehead and saw the moisture on her temples.

Dionis surfaced from a sea of pain. "I'm sorry," she gasped. "I . . . I feel dreadful. I think it's a tummy upset."

Frowning heavily, he picked up her limp wrist to feel her pulse and leaned forward to reach a compartment in the dashboard on her side of the car. "I have some brandy here. . . ."

"No . . . please," she managed. "I shall be better without anything at the moment. Please drive on. I'll be all right."

Her body was bathed in perspiration as a deadly nausea swept over her. One sip of the brandy and she felt sure she would have disgraced herself for ever by vomiting over the immaculate interior of the car.

Juan looked grim. Dolores and Rosalba leaned forward and he turned to speak to them. "Miss Ward is ill." He turned again to Dionis. "I'll be as quick as I can getting you back. If you feel too ill to sit you must lean against me and put your head on my shoulder."

He started the car with another swift look at Dionis, who lay back with closed eyes, hoping she could reach the inn before she passed out. The swift speed of the car, the intermittent pains in her stomach made the rest of the journey a nightmare. She was barely conscious when the car slid to a halt. The last thing she remembered was the faint pleasant aroma of cigars as Juan put his arms beneath her to carry her from the car.

CHAPTER VIII

THE next two days were ones Dionis was glad to see the end of. Pains tore through her like knives, leaving her head too woolly for coherent thought. Cool practised hands lifted her to give her pills or drinks and Doctor Horatio hovered in a mist of pain. On the third day she began to take notice of her surroundings, and found herself once again at the Villa Jacaranda.

"Mediterranean tummy, poor dear," Nurse Ford said. It was the initiation into the Spanish way of life. One had to experience it before becoming acclimatized. Nurse Ford had experienced it herself, so she could sympathize. Dionis, listless and wan, was beginning to think it was the worst thing she ever did to let Angela talk her into coming to Spain. Optimistically, Nurse Ford had brought her breakfast, a lightly boiled egg, some fingers of toast and cherry jam. Dionis managed two fingers of the toast. The day passed with Doctor Horatio calling in the afternoon, looking pleased at her progress. Juan was away on business and was expected back that evening. Dionis went to sleep about ten o'clock that night and awoke next morning feeling better. She ate her egg and toast and went for a shower. Some of her clothes had been sent from the inn and she put on a pale blue linen dress, deciding to wash her hair later on in the day when she felt up to it. Juan came about eleven. Dionis had a feeling he would come, for her nerves had been unsteady for some time before he strode in the room. Nurse Ford had gone to fetch her mid-morning drink and Dionis sat by the shuttered window doing her nails. She had a fragile paleness, but looked fresh and sweet.

"*Buenos dias*, Miss Ward. How are you?"

Don Juan gave her a thin smile which went nowhere near his eyes and she was sure he was more than fed up with the trouble she had caused him.

A warm flush crept beneath her clear skin to reach the roots of her hair where the heavy waves had been combed to frame her small face becomingly.

"Much better, thank you," she answered. He looked down at the pretty line of her neck, her small head held proudly and the sedate graceful way she sat, appraising the exquisite finish to every detail of her grooming which was part of her elusive charm. But it did not cover the shadowed eyes and wan look of exhaustion.

He said dryly, "I would say your independent spirit and not the feeling of wellbeing has forced you to leave your bed which you still need."

He stood with his back to the window, looking lithe and tanned with his dark hair catching the beams of sun filtering through the shutters. It was not until this moment that Dionis realized how much she had dreaded meeting him again.

She swallowed and plunged. "Being independent yourself, you will understand my anxiety to be up and about as soon as possible in order to relieve you of my presence. You must admit that I have caused you trouble one way or another since I arrived. Most of it has been my own fault too." She replaced the orange stick in her little manicure case, still avoiding his gaze.

There was a short silence during which he digested her remark, then said,

"You are merely going through a phase most visitors to this country experience at one time or another. The attack of sun, the sickness brought on by strange food — these things are sometimes unavoidable. And I can assure you that your presence in this house has been no trouble to anyone, least of all to myself. Nurse Ford has been in her element and has enjoyed looking after you." He paused significantly, his dark eyes very intent upon her bowed head. "There is one thing I would like to clear up. Dolores implied that the remarks I made about you being talented and clever would not be regarded as being very complimentary by a Spanish woman. What Dolores does not know is my first-hand knowledge of your countrymen which prompts me to talk to you as an Englishman would." A warmth crept into his voice. "Had I complimented you as a Spaniard you would have immediately put down my remarks as flattery. I admire courage and you appear to have a surfeit of it, plus a quality of dauntlessness which makes you a rare person." His eyes suddenly became mocking. "I also find you a very irresistible one."

Dionis lifted her head, giving him the benefit of her wide-eyed gaze. Her cheeks were softly flushed with sudden surprise and confusion, her smile hesitant.

"Thank you, señor," she said demurely. Her heart was beating like a sledgehammer as she encountered his eloquent eyes. "After all the trouble I've caused you to date, I consider that very noble of you."

He raised a brow, the mocking smile lingering in his eyes. "It was meant sincerely, I assure you."

"I don't doubt it." Dionis, drowning in his intent regard, pulled herself up sharply. "I feel much better today – well enough to make the journey back to the inn."

"The doctor is calling today. He is the one who will say when you are well enough to leave the villa. Unless I am mistaken, I can hear him now." He looked towards the door to see the doctor enter followed by Nurse Ford. "Buenos dias, Doctor," Juan said smoothly. "Had you been an hour or so later, I feel confident your patient would have gone. Miss Ward can hardly contain herself, so eager is she to return to the inn."

Doctor Horatio strode across the room to smile down on Dionis amiably. "It is good to see you up, señorita. How do you feel?"

He took her wrist between his fingers as he spoke and lifted an eyebrow at her quickened pulse. Dionis felt her colour deepen. Naturally he would put it down to the presence of the charming Don Juan, and she despised herself to know he would be right.

She avoided the glint in his eye. "The worst seems to be over and I feel much better this morning, Doctor – well enough to leave and return to the inn."

The doctor considered this. "Take my advice, *señorita,* and stay indoors today. The rest will do you good." Slowly he turned to Don Juan, releasing her wrist. "I would prescribe a run out in a car tomorrow for the *señorita.*" Don Juan nodded and the doctor patted her hand as it lay on the arm of her chair. "Do not be in too big a hurry to deprive people of the pleasure of your company. I leave you in good hands, so I shall not be calling to see you again. Take care of yourself, *señorita,* and enjoy your visit to our country. *Adios.*"

Nurse Ford carried a small table and put it down by Dionis. It contained a tray. On it was her mid-morning drink and small pastries.

"Try a pastry with your drink," Nurse Ford advised practically. "You will feel much better and you can afford to eat a few fattening foods with your slender figure. And now, if you will excuse me, I must fly. Doctor Horatio is calling to see my sister and I want to be there. This baby she's expecting is Spanish without a doubt. I never knew one so fond of taking his time at putting in an appearance! It would not surprise me if he did not grow up to be a bullfighter."

"Heaven forbid!" Dionis exclaimed, and Nurse Ford went out laughing.

At lunch time, Dionis ate a light meal of steamed fish, then slept right through the siesta. Later Rosalba came to take tea with her. Dolores had gone out with Juan. He did not call in to see her again that day, but Nurse Ford brought her a message from him with her breakfast the next morning. He was calling for her at ten-thirty to take her for a run in his car. Would she take a swim suit, he said, for he was taking her on a picnic.

No mention had been made of his sister or Dolores accompanying them and Dionis wondered if they had other plans. She hoped this was so. Surely to enjoy his company, quite intimately, in the short space of time which was hers in Spain, could be neither wrong nor dangerous. She found herself dressing with special care. Perhaps it was the sunshine, or her desire to go outdoors, or the natural feeling of wanting to look her best that made her glad the clothes sent from the inn included a rainbow-striped cotton dress with a soft yoke, yellow buttons and yellow patent leather belt. The yellow straw hat and matching sandals she had worn with her beach suit for her visit to Barcelona would go with it nicely.

Dionis awaited his arrival with a delicious expectancy. Nurse Ford had gone to see her sister. The baby had not yet arrived. She was waiting, standing ready with her beach bag when Juan came. Unaware that her confinement indoors had given her fragile prettiness a touching quality, Dionis turned to greet him.

His white silk shirt was open at the neck and a dark blue scarf was tucked neatly inside. The well tailored black jacket with its monogrammed pocket fitted snugly over his white slacks. He was too vibrantly masculine for any woman to relax completely in his presence, Dionis thought with dismay as with a charming smile he asked if she was fit enough to go on the outing. Picking up her beach bag, he went with her downstairs. After being in bed, her legs felt rather shaky, but the sight of his empty car sent her spirits soaring. At least she would not be bothered by the presence of Dolores.

An hour's run brought them within sight of the coast, passing villages to left, picturesque and dreaming against a background of purple hills. To her right a long white beach edged by sparkling blue sea gleamed invitingly. Presently, Juan ran the car off the road and on to a grass verge where they looked down on to the beach below. Apart from a handful of bathers at the far end of the cove the place was practically deserted. The air was deliciously tangy when she left the car and a soft warm wind whipped her dress against her slim figure.

Juan carried her beach bag and cupped her elbow to help her through the soft sand between dunes down to the beach.

"You can change here," he said, stopping at a pleasant

spot where overhanging rocks and high dunes topped by rough grass offered the maximum of privacy. He left her with a "See you in the water!" and disappeared around the rocks.

Standing alone beneath the vast shimmering blue sky with only the sound of the breakers on the shore, Dionis undressed, shedding not only her clothes but also the slack lethargic feeling following an illness. She found herself responding to the happiness of the morning as a flower responds to the sun. It amused her to think that Juan had taken it for granted that she could swim.

Impishly she hoped the English side of him would accept her bikini, a demure two-piece in turquoise. There was no sign of Juan when she walked along the beach to drop her towel on a dry patch of sand above the tide mark. The sea was warm and buoyant as she struck through it lazily, loving the feel of the water lapping over her limbs. Sensibly, she did not overtax her strength but turned on her back after swimming strongly for quite a distance to rest. How wonderful it was to be where only sun, sea and air mattered, with Don Juan!

Suddenly he was treading water beside her, slicking back his wet hair while drops of water clung to his black lashes and ran down his tanned face.

"Do not go out too far," he warned. "You are not a hundred per cent fit. Take care and do not stay in the water too long."

She nodded and he cleaved his way through the water with powerful strokes. When she was pleasantly tired, Dionis made for the beach. She had never felt self-conscious in a swim suit before, but she found herself hurrying to get to her short towelling jacket before Juan came out of the water. She belted it around her waist to show long slim legs and returned to where she had left her towel to find him already there. Clad in a towelling robe, he was opening a picnic basket.

His smile was white. "I hope you are hungry."

The next half hour was heaven to Dionis, who nibbled

chicken sandwiches and drank delicious coffee. Gradually conversation between them had ceased. Dionis did not know about Juan, but she was filled with a delicious languor. She lay back on the warm sand and watched him pack away the remains of their lunch and closed her eyes. Hours later she awakened to find Juan sitting beside her, supported by his hands. His dark eyes narrowed against the glare were concentrated on a ship well out to sea. There was something indicative of waiting in his attitude, something Spanish in his immobility, in his entire absorption of the view before him. Dionis tried not to be so aware of him and failed to be as indifferent as he appeared to be. His personality was such that it was impossible to ignore his presence. She felt relieved that he appeared not bored but detached from his present surroundings. As if aware of her watching him, he turned his head to smile down on her.

"Ready for a drink? We have a full flask of coffee in reserve."

"Lovely," she answered, and sat up eagerly.

Without more ado he was pouring out two steaming cups of coffee and offering her one. Sitting there in the shade of the rocks drinking her coffee, Dionis gave herself up to the joy of the moment with sensuous abandon. Watching the clean-cut line of his jaw, the line of brutality in it, she felt instinctively that his relaxed attitude was that of a man too full of life to be restless. In those quiet moments the male in him seized and dominated her with a curious thrill of pleasure. She sensed the danger and finishing her coffee said it was time she dressed.

She dressed swiftly in the hollow in the sand dunes, but took care with her make-up. In the small mirror her face glowed and her eyes were clear and shining. She was in no way as dark and luscious as Dolores and she wondered if Juan was of the same opinion. Dionis tried to be realistic about him. Bringing her out today meant nothing more to him than taking out a guest. He was not likely to follow it up with other invitations. It occurred to her painfully that the outing was meant to hasten her convalescence in order to give him more time with Dolores. Well, the sooner the better. His masculine charm was far too lethal.

Juan, fully dressed and almost immaculate, leaned against a huge rock smoking a cigar when she emerged from the shelter of the sand dunes. His dark hair had dried crisply and his tanned features glowed from his sojourn in the sun. Straightening, he dropped his cigar, ground his heel into it and taking her beach bag walked with her to the car. Sitting beside him, Dionis watched the road ahead twist and turn beneath his superb guidance. Dark shadows beneath trees changed to dazzling light as they emerged to scenes of distant hills where the outline of old trees stood out grotesquely like abstract paintings.

He was the first to break the silence. "My sister and her friend are out visiting friends for the day. As they will not return in time for dinner I wondered if you would mind dining alone with me."

Dionis hesitated. She had given no thought to the evening. He spoke as though it was an understood thing for her to dine with them all that evening. But to dine alone with him? The very air quivered with crisis. Well, why not? Why should she not hoard felicity against the time when it would be no more?

He was swift to interpret her glance down at her dress. "It is not necessary for you to go to the inn to change. The little dress you are wearing will do. We shall not stand on ceremony."

The first thing Dionis saw when she went to her room at the Villa Jacaranda was a note propped up on the dressing table. It was from Nurse Ford to say that her sister had been taken with labour pains and it seemed that the little bullfighter was on the way. She could not say when she would be back. Dionis smiled happily for Nurse Ford's sister and hoped everything would be all right after her long wait. She did not need Nurse Ford again herself in any case. She walked to the window and pushed open the shutters, filling her lungs with the evening air. Loving the unidentifiable fragrance, she stared in front of her unseeingly. She had set out on her career with the firm conviction that happiness lay in self-fulfilment. Most women sought it in love and marriage. She had wanted to find it in her career. On the whole, her life had been full and rewarding. Her complete absorption in her job, the excitement of each new assignment challenging her skill had swept her along from one week to another on a wave of enthusiasm and joy. When well-meaning friends had introduced her to eligible young men none had been as important to her as her job.

Was it only yesterday that she had wanted to go back to the inn so desperately? Now the opportunity had arisen for her to do so. Why was she so reluctant? The moment of truth was like a jigsaw falling in to place. She loved Juan. It was not possible for her not to love him. The hours she had spent with him today had been filled with a divine rapture, a contentment hitherto unknown. From their first meeting he had all the charm and excitement of a completely new experience for her. No man had roused her emotions in the way he had. If she had paused to analyse them she would have known without a doubt. Slowly, Dionis lifted shaking hands to her flushed cheeks. Facing the truth with an absolute and final certainty, she felt stunned. Of course, she knew exactly what the position was – how hopeless. Not only was he far above her socially, he was more or less already betrothed to Dolores. There was only one thing to do – freeze out her hopeless yearning for a love which could never be hers, leave the Villa Jacaranda as soon as possible and carry on with her work. When she had finished at the Villa Acacia, she would go home and never look back.

But that evening as she washed and changed to dine with him, Dionis could not banish the sweet exhilarating thought that soon she would be seeing him and talking to him again. Nurse Ford had not put in an appearance when it was time for her to go downstairs. A manservant hovered in the hall. Her heart was gyrating somewhere near her throat, giving her the urge to continue down the stairs and out through the front door away from new and disturbing emotions she had no idea to suppress. Flags of colour stained her cheeks when he stepped forward to show her into the dining room to see Juan pouring out drinks.

He was wearing a dark lounge suit and gave her a smile of extraordinary charm. *"Buenas tardes,* Miss Ward. Not too tired after your picnic?" The dark eyes rested upon her flushed face and over-bright eyes politely.

Her heart was slowing down to normal, but her legs felt as if they were not her own as she sat in the chair he drew forward. She accepted the drink, trying to borrow some of his superb confidence.

"Not at all. I enjoyed it immensely. I shall sleep well to-night." Dionis looked down into her glass and saw that it was champagne. "Did you know Nurse Ford had gone to her sister? It seems the baby is due."

He smiled down at her drink in hand, and it came to her that this was how she would remember him, standing apart from all his wealth and family. Not as a figment of her romantic dreams, a Prince Charming, but as a man, the only man to win her heart.

"Yes, I knew. What do you say to drinking to the baby?" Dionis raised her glass with a curious ache in her heart. "To the little bullfighter."

He raised a brow but drank the toast. "You are sure it is going to be a boy?"

"Nurse Ford appears to think so, because the baby is so slow in arriving."

"And a girl would be more on time?"

"It's generally believed to be so," she said demurely.

He laughed, noting her blush. "Are you fond of children, Miss Ward?"

Dionis swallowed, imagining the utter joy of having his children, chided herself for being a fool and answered calmly, "I love them."

"They are certainly essential to a happy marriage. Tell me . . ."

He was interrupted by a knock on the door and a man-servant entered at his bidding. "Señor Delusi to see you, *señor*," he said.

Juan frowned at the unfamiliar name. But Dionis was slowly rising to her feet to put down her half-finished drink with trembling fingers. A slim man of medium height whose olive complexion, black hair and handsome features stamped him unmistakably as a Latin entered the room. Wearing a smart city-going suit, he strode across the room to where she now stood, his face alight with pleasure.

"Dionis! What is this about you being ill?" He kissed her on both cheeks, then looked at her anxiously. "You are better? Señor Lopez at the inn told me you were here ill in bed."

Dionis drew a deep breath of pleasure mingled with surprise. "I was, Mediterranean tummy, but I've quite recovered. Whatever are you doing here?"

He rolled brown eyes in mock dismay. "What am I doing here, she asks? Don't you remember? I said I would call to see you on my way to the exhibition in Madrid." Before Dionis could reply, Cesare became aware of the silent figure of Don Juan. "I beg your pardon, *señor*, for butting in like this. I was concerned about my little friend." His frown was speculative. "Have we not met before at an exhibition in Madrid?"

"Possibly," was the cool reply.

Dionis said hurriedly, "Cesare, may I present Señor Juan Stebelo. He owns the Villa Acacia which I have the pleasure of decorating. *Señor*, my former employer, Cesare Delusi, who taught me all I know about interior decorating."

The two men shook hands. "Delighted to meet you, *señor*," Cesare said warmly. "I'm pleased someone is keeping an eye on Dionis." His smile at her was fond. "As for me teaching her, she is a natural at her job. But thank heaven she is not one of those self-sufficient career women who know it all. I can't bear the breed. They go through life like well-coiffured bulldozers. Not Dionis." His fingers touched her flushed cheek with Latin charm. "She is good for a man's ego."

Dionis, happy to see her old friend, dimpled deliciously.

"I am afraid the *señor* would not agree with you. I've been an awful nuisance to him since I arrived."

Juan did not answer. He was pouring out a drink for his unexpected visitor. "Please sit down, Signor Delusi," he said politely, handing him the glass. "You are staying to dine with us, of course."

"Thanks, *señor*. I should be delighted, if it is not inconvenient."

Again Juan did not answer. He merely excused himself and strode from the room.

"Have I interrupted something?" Cesare asked, taking a chair near to Dionis. "Your host seemed rather distant, though charmingly polite."

Dionis sat down weakly, watching him take down part of his drink. "Good heavens, no!" she answered a shade too emphatically. "Don Juan and I are not exactly close. Rather the reverse." She wrinkled a pretty nose. "Not only does he heartily disapprove of me, he also disapproves of me decorating the Villa Acacia. Angela's fiancé, who rents it from him, didn't see fit to tell him about it. He and Don Juan are distantly related."

"In more ways than one, it seems," Cesare said dryly. He leaned back in his chair and looked at her thoughtfully. "Does that mean there's a deadlock?"

"On the contrary. Don Juan has been most helpful." Dionis went on to tell him all that had occurred.

"So you are now waiting for your materials to arrive," he said when he had finished. "Those you ordered in Barcelona should not take so long as the bulk of them from London. In that case I shall be able to help you to get the small jobs done. I don't suppose I shall be here when the other arrives." He raised a brow query-wise. "You are going to the exhibition in Madrid next week?"

"Of course. As a matter of fact, I've been looking forward to it. I told you the exhibition was one of the reasons I accepted this job of decorating the Villa Acacia. It's just that. . . ." Dionis broke off, made a futile gesture with a feeling she was not very convincing. "Well, things have been happening to push it completely from my mind."

If Cesare thought this an odd remark coming from a young woman who hitherto had thought of nothing but her job, he made no comment. But his pleasant brown eyes narrowed across at her slightly before he tossed off the rest of his drink.

CHAPTER IX

THE next day saw Dionis back at the inn where Cesare had booked a room. Señora Lopez had taken him in when he explained about his reason for being there. The materials Dionis had ordered from Barcelona had arrived and Cesare went with her to the Villa Acacia. There she outlined her intentions and he insisted upon carrying them out while she looked on. He appraised everything she had in mind and made great friends with Paco. Dionis had not seen Juan since the evening she had dined with him and Cesare. He had not been at the villa the next morning when she left, but one of his cars had been put at her disposal. Rosalba and Dolores had not been in evidence neither.

With Cesare to help, Dionis concentrated on the job in hand. His approval of her plans had lifted her spirits and given her the confidence she needed. A letter came from Angela, who was obviously in high spirits. She asked how Dionis was faring at the villa and mentioned that Tony would write later. Dionis wrote back one evening saying nothing of Juan, but she did say that Cesare had called while on a visit to the exhibition in Madrid.

Dear Cesare, she thought, pausing pen in hand. His presence had helped considerably in putting Juan out of her thoughts. Any future assignments in Spain would be out. She would leave when the job was done never to return. Erasing Juan from her life would not be easy. He had carved too deep a niche in it for it to be entirely obliterated. But her job was a great tranquillizer.

She accompanied Cesare to Madrid the following week. They put up at a hotel for three nights, spending their days around the exhibition, their evenings dancing or going to shows. Cesare was in high spirits, finding himself reunited with old acquaintances at the exhibition with whom he chatted while Dionis wandered around making notes of various interesting exhibits. On these occasions Dionis would find herself looking for Don Juan's immaculate figure. He had been to previous exhibitions, it was possible that he might attend this one. Each time she saw the back of a lean athletic figure walking arrogantly, her heart lurched. She looked in vain.

When she returned to the inn with Cesare a letter awaited her. The order for materials from London had been dispatched and was due to arrive the following day. The next day the workmen Don Juan had promised arrived simultaneously with Dionis wondering how he knew for she had not contacted him. Cesare, with a fortnight of his holiday still to go, stayed for a week to help Dionis at the Villa Acacia before going on to his family in Italy. With Cesare in charge everything went smoothly. He had the knack of getting the best out of his workmen. When he left at the end of the week, work at the villa was well under way with Dionis contacting the village seamstress Juan had recommended for the curtains and soft furnishings.

Dionis had written to her sister, Angela, informing her of her progress, intimating that the job was nearing completion. Angela had replied to say she would be happy if Dionis would stay on for a while until she knew the definite date they would return. As yet it was uncertain. Dionis received the news with dismay, wanting no delays to keep her in Spain when the job was done. Immediately she wrote back asking for a definite date as every week away from her job in London was important.

So the days passed with Dionis absorbed in her job at the villa. Most nights she felt too weary to eat her late meal, but at least she was tired out enough to sleep the moment her head touched the pillow. She derived great comfort from the companionship of Don Fernando, who came to the inn each evening for his glass of wine and cigar. On the brazier-warmed patio, Dionis would sit and talk with him while she waited for her meal at ten. He told her about her father, his likes and dislikes, bringing him so near in spirit that his presence was almost tangible. She had become used, now, to the beauty and natural simplicity of the people her father had loved. His ties with them were ties which could bind her also — but she must not think about it. It was Don Fernando who told her of the arrival of Nurse Ford's sister's baby.

"It is a fine boy, the image of his father. You have not been to see him yet? Nurse will be leaving any time now. Nice woman."

"Yes, she is. I must go to see her before she leaves to thank her for looking after me when I was ill. I'm so glad about the baby." Dionis coloured a little self-consciously. "I've been meaning to go, but I've been so busy of late."

Don Fernando leaned forward to pat her hand. "Never be too busy to visit your friends. You know the saying about all work and no play. You have lost your sparkle, niña. Take a day away from your work. You will return much refreshed."

But not happy, Dionis thought bitterly. She longed to ask for news of Juan, but was afraid of betraying her feeling for him if she did. On this particular evening, Fernando was in a confiding mood, however.

"Don Juan has taken his sister and her friend back to Cadiz. Speculation is high as to whether he will marry the señorita, who has known him since they were children together. It is expected that he will marry soon, because his sister is getting married at the end of the year. Juan will miss her playing hostess to his guests when he entertains. Doña Rosalba will be married in the cathedral in Madrid. Her novio is a member of a wealthy aristocratic family and the wedding will be a big event." He imparted the news with an enigmatic expression directed at the cigar he held motionless in his hand. Then carefully he tapped off the long accumulation of ash into an ash tray provided nearby on a low table. "You would enjoy the wedding, and you are quite welcome to come and stay with us if you care to, niña. My wife and I have become very attached to you."

So Rosalba was getting married. Dionis felt her heart lurch painfully as she pictured Dolores as bridesmaid looking provocatively up at Juan in the muted light of the lovely old cathedral. In Cadiz he would be rocking women's hearts with his charming smile, driving the big car at speed along white roads taking Rosalba and his intended on visits to villas similar to their own. Dining on patios or in cool shuttered rooms, Dionis could imagine him smiling tenderly, mockingly on Dolores, enchanted by her beauty, the dainty movements of her expressive hands, her feminine laughter and excited chatter. Dionis Ward would be as far away from his thoughts as he was miles away from her.

"Thank you," she said. "How kind you are. I am fond of you too. It has meant a great deal to me to know you knew and loved my father. It will always be a bond between us. Maybe one day I shall come back, but not, I think, at the end of the year. By then I shall be up to the ears in work." Dionis swallowed on a lump in her throat seeking to hide her unhappiness from Don Fernando. "I am a working woman."

"Do not work too hard, *niña*. Work will be there when you are gone. Enjoy yourself when you can."

After her siesta the following afternoon, Dionis, mindful of Don Fernando's advice, decided to go to see Nurse Ford. The men could work on their own now at the Villa Acacia without consulting her. She waited at the bus stop outside the inn planning to call at the post office in the village for a present for the new baby. On her last visit, Dionis remembered a pretty box decorated with cherubs and blue ribbon that she had seen there. Prettily packed, beneath the transparent wrapping there was a baby's brush and comb, rattle, soap and baby powder and a small duck to float upon the bath water. Dionis was thinking about it when the car slid to a stop in front of her.

"Can I give you a lift, *señorita?*" Doctor Horatio asked with smiling Spanish courtesy.

"If it won't take you out of your way," she answered lightly. "I'm on my way to the Villa Jacaranda."

He raised a brow. "I happen to be going that way myself. I was not aware that Don Juan had returned to take up residence there."

He had opened the door of his car and Dionis slid in beside him as he spoke.

"I'm going to see Nurse Ford and the baby," she said.

"Then you are bound for Lemon Tree Cottage like myself. Nurse Ford is with her sister and her husband in the small cottage at the end of the drive leading to the Villa Jacaranda. Don Juan gave them the place when he heard about the baby. He thought they would be happier in a place of their own instead of living in at the Villa Jacaranda. The birth was not an easy one and the baby has had difficulty in taking his food."

"Poor mite," Dionis said sympathetically. "I hope it's nothing serious."

"As the mother is feeding him herself I am of the opinion that her milk is a little rich. He appears to be thriving on it, though, and it is the surest way of bringing up a healthy child."

Soon they reached the village, when the doctor waited in the car while Dionis went into the post office for the baby's present. She had looked up her Spanish and was able to ask unfalteringly for the present she had in mind. Joy spread across the rather sombre expression of the postmistress when Dionis stated her request. Watching her small hands flutter birdlike over the shelves behind her to rest eventually on the pretty box, Dionis smiled. Shopping in Spain was certainly not the businesslike affair it was in London. The *señora* agreed on it being an ideal present for a baby and brought down from the shelf another little box containing a woolly matinée jacket in white with blue ribbons. Dionis bought that too. Two women drifted in while the postmistress looked round for wrappings. At last, somewhat reluctantly, so it seemed to Dionis, the presents were wrapped, but not before the two newcomers had purred over them with ecstatic murmurings. A new baby was a popular topic in any language, she mused. All this had taken time which could not be avoided, and Dionis emerged from the shop hoping the doctor was still waiting. He was, patiently. No doubt he knew how long it would take her.

Lemon Tree Cottage was a whitewashed, green-roofed building with blue shutters. Everywhere in the garden there were flowers, bougainvillea, hydrangeas, white, yellow and red roses, all scattering their scent on the warm air. The front of the cottage which caught the morning shade now slumbered in the shade with the shutters open to the view. Stopping the car a short distance away from the cottage in case the baby was asleep, the doctor walked with Dionis towards the rose-covered porch. Suddenly he paused, and Dionis followed the direction of his gaze. Inside the cottage in a room to the left of the porch a woman was clearly visible silhouetted against the white walls. She held the baby in her arms and was lowering it gently inside a very pretty cot. The woman was Don Fernando's sister, Pilar. Taking in the scene, Dionis wondered how she could have thought the woman plain and uninteresting. Pilar's expression was so tender and sweet, so filled with love that Dionis felt a rough lump in her throat. As she looked down tenderly upon the sleeping child, Pilar positively glowed with a hidden beauty which she had been privileged to see.

This new aspect of a woman who held such a capacity for making some man gloriously happy filled Dionis with disgust that men could be so blind. Sighing audibly with exasperation as they turned away, she found the doctor smiling down at her benignly.

"Tired, *señorita*?" he asked.

"Goodness, no. Entranced is more like it. What a beautiful picture Doña Pilar made with the child in her arms."

He nodded. "So you noticed it too. Every woman should have at least one child. It is her natural birthright and the supreme fulfilment of her womanhood."

Dionis said dryly, "Pity Doña Pilar is to be denied that privilege. How unfortunate she is to be among men who go about in blinkers, so blind that they cannot see the prize beneath their nose."

Nurse Ford met them in the porch. "*Buenas tardes, doc-*

tor," she exclaimed. "You've missed my sister by minutes. Her husband has taken her to see his mother, who has been taken ill rather suddenly. Baby has just been fed and he's much better. Doña Pilar has come to tea and is putting him in his cot."

"*Bien,*" the doctor nodded. "I will take a look at him. I promise not to wake him."

He strode indoors in the manner of a man who knew his way about and Nurse Ford gave her attention to Dionis.

"Do come in." She led the way indoors. "You appear to have recovered from your illness and are no doubt now fully acclimatized." Her eyes twinkled mischievously, as she added, "We hope!" She gestured Dionis to a comfortable chair in a room which charmed her on sight. "Do sit down while I make tea. I don't know about you, but I'm dying for a cup."

Nurse Ford left the room and Dionis looked round at a charming room. The ceiling was in pale blue with traceries of gold. The colours were repeated in the faded blue and primrose-tiled floor covered by a circular rug in pastel colours. The shutters were closed, giving the impression that the room looked out on to the back garden open to the afternoon and evening sun. Fingers of light stiffly spread pushed their way in between the shutters gleaming richly on brass vases, and bowls filled with simple flower arrangements, while dark well-polished furniture gleamed mellowly against white walls. There was a restful, happy atmosphere pervading the air and Dionis loved it.

The doctor entered, his broad shoulders giving the room much smaller proportions. He was followed by Pilar, looking decidedly flushed. As for the doctor, Dionis thought he looked ten years younger and very boyish as he smiled down at her.

"It is my half day off from duty. I shall be passing this way in about an hour and a half. I should be delighted to give you two *señoritas* a lift home."

"That would be lovely. Do you not think so, Doña Pilar?" Dionis turned a bright smile on Pilar, who nodded shyly. Why not? thought Dionis. Each would be a chaperone for the other, all perfectly correct. "*Gracias*, doctor," she said.

"Would you like to see the baby, Miss Ward?"

The doctor had left and Pilar led the way to the nursery.

Dionis sighed ecstatically. "Isn't he delicious?" she whispered, bending over the cot admiring the chubby cheeks, rosebud mouth and tiny dimpled hands.

"*Precioso*," murmured Pilar, nodding her head and smiling. The tender expression was again on her face and Dionis hoped with all her heart that the doctor had contributed to the happiness in her eyes. It was a bit disappointing for Nurse Ford if she liked the man. She looked anything but disappointed, though, when she carried in the tea. "Have you seen the baby?" she asked brightly. "Isn't he a poppet?" She put down the tray and set about pouring tea. "I shall hate leaving him, but I've overstayed my time already."

Three heads, a black one, a brown one and a chestnut one, bobbed up and down in delighted conversation as they ate the daintily prepared tea. A mounting exhilaration filled Dionis as she laughed gaily at the amusing stories Nurse Ford trotted out of life in a big London hospital. The tea, prolonged with animated conversation, came reluctantly to an end when the sound of a car was heard stopping outside. The doctor was on time. While Nurse Ford went to answer the door Dionis and Pilar prepared to leave. They were standing when Nurse Ford returned with the visitor. Dionis caught her breath in her throat as she recognised the deep familiar voice before the owner promptly appeared.

"So, I have missed Fabrique and his charming wife." Juan was speaking to Nurse Ford in English. "No matter. I have a rather important packet which I wanted to give Fabrique myself. You will see that he receives it the moment he returns, *por favor*?"

As they entered the room he gave Nurse Ford a long bulky envelope. Then he was greeting Pilar in Spanish, resorting again to English when his dark eyes rested upon Dionis. At once she was vividly aware of his presence and instantly reponsive to it. Her observation, sharpened by love, took in every detail of his appearance, the dark eyes which could sparkle with mockery or shut her out with glints of steel, his superb carriage and strength of character.

He addressed her formally. "I trust you have fully recovered from your illness, Miss Ward. Perhaps the visit to the exhibition in Madrid with your friend did much to hasten your recovery." Inexorably, with just the right degree of politeness, he erected a wall between them, topped, Dionis felt, by broken glass. The dark eyes had narrowed, the sharply cut nostrils had thinned. "You appeared to be enjoying yourself when I saw you there."

So he had been to the exhibition after all. And he had left without making his presence known to her. How could he? The revelation came as a blow below the belt. Dionis bit on a quivering lip.

"I ... I had no idea you would be going," she said on breath regained.

He was still unsmiling. "Naturally, as the owner of property, I keep abreast with the times." His eyes rested for a brief second on her unadorned left hand. "How is work progressing at the Villa Acacia?"

"Very well. Thanks for sending the workmen," she said woodenly.

"I kept a promise," he replied coldly. Then he raised a brow on seeing the three women standing. "Have I interrupted anything?"

"I ... we ... Doña Pilar and I are just leaving," Dionis stammered.

"Then may I offer to escort you *señoritas* home? My visit here is fleeting. I am on my way back to Cadiz and can drop you on my way."

Dionis had visions of the doctor on his way to pick them up. She could only surmise that Doctor Horatio was interested in Pilar as a woman. One swift glance at the *señorita's* impassive face told her nothing. But there was something there that struck Dionis to the heart — a hopeless resignation, an acceptance of a fate which was intent on thwarting all possibility of her ever reaching the altar on some man's arm. There are some moments in life which can alter its whole course for good or ill. Dionis felt this was such a moment for Pilar Peralta. She thought of Doctor Horatio, almost boyish as he offered them a lift home. If they went now with Don Juan the doctor would be hurt. He might even think Pilar had accepted Juan's lift in an effort to avoid him. If he did pride would seal his lips. He would never make his feelings known to the *señorita*.

Dionis lifted eyes eloquent with the poignancy of the situation. "That's very kind of you. But we're waiting for a friend who is calling to pick us up." Her voice was almost inaudible. "We couldn't disappoint him."

His small bow was given with a touch of hauteur. Juan was not accustomed to being refused when he graciously offered two ladies a lift.

"Naturally," he said stiffly. Then with a lithe movement characteristic of him he was addressing Nurse Ford. "Give my regards to the *señor* and the *señora*. You will not forget to give him the package?"

"He shall have it the moment he returns," Nurse Ford assured him.

"*Gracias.* I hope his mother recovers soon. *Adios*, nurse, Doña Pilar, Miss Ward." Another stiff little bow and he was gone.

"Well, well!" Nurse Ford exclaimed with her usual frankness when he had gone. "Here was I wishing I was staying at the inn or somewhere which would necessitate a car ride. To think of sitting beside Don Juan in that fabulous car on an evening such as this! Why, anything could happen!" She sighed goodhumouredly. "Good thing I shall soon be back on the daily grind. A dish like Don Juan can certainly fill your head with all kinds of romantic notions. He's fabulous! He's given the baby a whopping cheque which will go towards his education when the time comes. Isn't it sweet of him?"

But Dionis was beyond words. She had snubbed the man and he was not likely to forget it. Doctor Horatio arrived soon after with Nurse Ford waving them off from the porch When the doctor opened the back door of the car for the two women to sit in the back, Dionis put on her brightest smile.

"Do sit in front with the doctor, Doña Pilar. I shall be getting out before you and you will be company for each other."

They made a charming couple, the *señorita* so sweet, so feminine, and the doctor so broad, strong and protective. So thought Dionis as she looked upon them fondly from the back seat. Somehow she knew that everything female inside her had assessed the situation truly. It only needed a situation like this with Pilar's narrow shoulder touching his powerful one plus the closed intimacy of the car for him to tell her of his feelings for her. With this in mind, she strove to establish a cordiality between them by chatting amiably and airing her Spanish. Dionis was happy to see them both relaxed when she alighted at the inn and keeping her fingers crossed for Pilar, she waved gaily and went indoors.

Señora Lopez met her at the foot of the stairs. "Don Juan called earlier to see the extension at the back of the inn now that it is finished. He asked about you. As a matter of fact you only missed him by about an hour. He did not ask after Señor Delusi, so I did not inform him of the *señor*'s departure."

Dionis told Señora Lopez of her visit to see Nurse Ford and the baby and her meeting with Juan. Señora Lopez wanted to hear all about the baby, of course. Later, going up to her room, it occurred to Dionis again what Señora Lopez had said about Cesare leaving the inn. If Juan did not know of his departure he would probably think it was Cesare who was giving Pilar and herself a lift home from Lemon Tree Cottage. His sudden glance at her left hand convinced her of his belief that there was something between her and Cesare, much more than friendship. What did it matter? Pushing her hair back wearily from her face,

Dionis realized that this afternoon's encounter with him might well be her last before she left Spain. He had said he was returning to Cadiz. There would be no reason for him to return for a long time now that the extension to the inn was finished. In that moment the pain in her heart was more than she could bear at the thought that she had seen him for the last time. Closing the door of her room, she walked slowly towards the little pot in which she had planted his posy of forget-me-nots. They were thriving, and as she bent over them the tears fell.

CHAPTER X

THE day had begun like any other day at the inn. Dionis had arisen early, showered and donned her working attire, slacks and a pretty top and gone down to breakfast. Señora Lopez brought her breakfast this morning. Tercia had gone with her father to pay a duty visit to his parents. There was a letter for Dionis in the morning's post from Angela. Dionis began her breakfast intending to read it later. She had not opened it when Señora Lopez brought fresh coffee at the end of her meal.

"Stay and have a cup with me, *señora*," Dionis said with a smile. "I shall not have many more mornings here."

Señora Lopez shook her head regretfully. "Not this morning, *gracias*. I have too much to do. I will leave you to read your letter. Later, perhaps, you would like to see the new extension. We stayed up until well into the early hours this morning putting it to rights. Don Juan was very pleased with it when he saw it last evening. So modern too."

Dionis allowed the last remark to pass over her head. "I'd love to see it, *señora*."

Over the fragrant coffee Dionis picked up Angela's letter and casually slit it open. The next instant she was staring at it in horror. The written words danced before her eyes as she tried to take in their meaning.

"Dear Dionis," she read, "the party is over. Tony and I have parted for good."

It was some time before Dionis could continue reading the letter. Her face was ashen when she eventually read on. Angela went on to say that the parting was final. Experienced though she was with men, her instinct had failed to warn her of the hint of coarseness and sensuality in her fiancé's character. Had she not been so infatuated with him she would have seen his habitual self-indulgence in the slackness of his mouth. He had lied to her, for she had discovered that he had no money or prospects, having gone through a fortune left to him by his stepfather, a distant cousin of Juan's. Her fiancé had no scruples and was going through a shady deal in property in Bermuda, and that to Angela was the last straw. In short Antonio was a completely selfish lover with the makings of the worst kind of husband. When Dionis received this letter she would be on her way back to London to ask for her job back. Rather callously, Angela ended by advising Dionis to get out of the mess as best she could.

With the feeling that she had aged ten years in the last few minutes, Dionis put down the letter with a sinking heart. Had she made a mistake in not telling Angela that her fiancé was already engaged to someone else? It was questionable whether she would have taken heed. How long Dionis sat there she never knew. But when her brain began to function again her first thought was for the workmen at the Villa Acacia. Had Antonio enough money in his account to pay them, for their contract was nearly finished? Dionis had forwarded the bills for the materials to his bank and had so far received no reply. Well, no news was good news. Even so, for her own peace of mind she had to contact his bank to make sure. Beyond that Dionis dared not think.

Maintaining a warm enthusiastic front when later Señora Lopez escorted her around the new extension to the inn was one of the hardest things Dionis had ever known. She had a vague impression of a sparkling modern kitchen, an intriguing cocktail bar and a sun lounge. It had evidently been designed by a first-class architect. The décor, brilliantly done, was exotic yet restrained by virtue of attention to detail. Normally, Dionis would have looked on it with pleasure, ever alert to learn from first-class designers. But a sense of fatality held her rigid, an inner confusion jumbled thoughts with which she wrestled in vain.

Fortunately Señora Lopez, thrilled with the new premises and a future bright with hope, noticed nothing. When Dionis asked permission to use the phone in her small office later, Señora Lopez left her there and closed the door behind her. With a wildly beating heart, Dionis contacted the operator and was put through to the bank in Barcelona. There were anxious moments until his voice came through and she waited while he went in search of Antonio's bank account. "*Si*," he said. Two bills had been settled by the bank, one for an order of materials from Barcelona, the other, a much bigger one, from London. Unfortunately, the last bill had left a small overdraft. He was trying to contact *el señor* in Bermuda about it. If the *señorita* would ring him again towards the end of the week, he might have some news for her.

Sick at heart, Dionis agreed to do this and slowly put down the receiver. The men would have to be paid, if it meant drawing what money she had in the bank. It was then she began to realize that the problem was not hers alone. It was also Juan's. The Villa Acacia was his property and he had a right to know what had happened. He would find out eventually in any case. So with a heavy heart, Dionis wrote him a note to say it was imperative for her to see him at his earliest convenience. She addressed it to the Villa Jacaranda and went out to post it on her way to the Villa Acacia. Nothing would be gained by calling a halt to work there which was due to be completed in a matter of days. Dionis worked hard at the villa, staying long after the workmen left each evening and returning to the inn too tired and too dispirited to enjoy her evening meal.

Mid-week, she received two letters. One was from Nurse Ford's sister thanking her for the baby's present and asking her to call any time she felt inclined. The other was from Don Fernando requesting her presence at a dinner party to be given at the Villa Inez. The occasion was the engagement of his sister Pilar to Doctor Horatio de Quexeri. It was the one bright spot in her dark world – so thought Dionis with a tender smile. If she had been instrumental in bringing those two delightful people together then she did not regret her own foolishness in coming to Spain.

She dressed with special care for the event in a dress of

crisp white organdie flecked with blue. The silver belt around her slim waist matched her slippers and evening bag. Her hair was soft and bright around her small face, but Dionis felt no joy in her own attractive reflection, only a humble thankfulness for this brief period of respite that released her for a few hours from tormenting thoughts. It was an anodyne, deadening the pain in her heart as she longed yet dreaded to see Juan again.

With Doña Inez, Don Fernando greeted her warmly. They were obviously as delighted as she was about the engagement. Then Pilar was there.

"You look very lovely," she said to Dionis, radiant herself in black lace. Happiness had brought a new beauty to her face.

"So do you, Doña Pilar," she replied. "May I see your ring?"

Taking Pilar's fingers to admire the great emerald flashing in the light, Dionis felt the small fingers curling around her own. "It's beautiful," she breathed. "Congratulations, Doña Pilar. I know you are going to be very happy with your nice doctor." Their eyes met in perfect understanding and Dionis gave the *señorita*'s fingers an answering squeeze.

Guests drifted in and everyone was genuinely delighted to be present on such a happy occasion. Later, over dinner, Dionis saw the happy couple engrossed in each other in the manner of a couple very much in love. After the protracted meal finally ended, Dionis found an opportunity to congratulate the doctor.

"I am delighted that two such nice people have found their happiness in each other. Doña Pilar is a perfect pet. You are a very lucky *hombre*, Doctor Horatio," she said.

"*Gracias, señorita,*" he answered gravely. "I trust that some day you will find the same happiness."

"*Gracias,*" Dionis said with a gaiety she was far from feeling. Love had come to her, but she would never drink from its cup of happiness. Only Juan had the power to offer it to her, and he would not want to know her again after what she had to tell him.

The happy evening drew gently to its close with Dionis feeling like Cinderella returning to a life of care. She was given a lift back to the inn by a charming couple. Dionis thanked them and made her way across the silent courtyard of the inn where long shadows lay chequered in the moonlight. From beneath the shade of the lemon trees, she looked towards the patio lit by the dying glow of the brazier. Her heart moved oddly in her breast, she held her breath as deep emotion held her spellbound. It was a mixture of joy and sorrow, laughter and tears, ecstasy and utter desolation as she came unawares upon the beloved figure that haunted her dreams.

Juan was leaning nonchalantly against one of the pillars upholding the patio. Dionis stared at him, the feeling inside her banished by the enormity of what she had to tell him. Her feeling for him had not changed. It was not infatuation that she felt for him. It could only be love making her whole being reach out to him, filling her with the premonitory pain unrequited love brought in its wake. He had seen her, of course, alerted by the sound of the car putting her down at the gates.

Dionis had no recollection of crossing the courtyard. Only the dark enigmatic face of Juan was before her, drawing her to him. She was herself a ghost, transparent as the crisp white organdie which frothed about her like evening mist. Her silver slippers made barely a sound and the perfume of trees and flowers seemed to be overwhelming.

"My faith!" he breathed, straightening slowly as if any sudden movement on his part might cause her to vanish. "Did you come on a moonbeam?" With a smile startlingly white in the dimness, he was aware suddenly of her pale, unsmiling face. She was like a ghost to which the unreality of the evening had given a spurious vitality. His smile faded. "I received your note. You are in trouble, Miss Ward?"

Slowly, Dionis raised her eyes until they met his full and straight. She forced the words out, determined to be frank, although they threatened to choke her. Her voice was barely above a whisper.

"I'm sorry," she began. "Something dreadful has happened. My sister Angela has broken off her engagement to . . . to Antonio."

Then, because her legs felt incapable of supporting her, Dionis sat down on the seat by the wall of the patio.

He digested the news in silence for several moments. At last, frowning deeply, he said, "What is going to happen now?"

Dionis did not immediately understand him. "What do you mean?"

He gave an alien shrug and thrust his hands into his pockets. "Now that the engagement is broken, is there no chance of a reconciliation?"

"None." She shook her head. "Angela is adamant. She has broken the engagement because she's of the opinion that Antonio would make a very unsatisfactory husband."

He stared at her with that curious, baffling reserve which, while it intrigued, also served to fill her with foreboding. The patio was warm from the still glowing brazier, but there was a distinct nip in the evening air.

"This is very interesting," The dark eyes narrowed. In the dim light his face was set and stern. "Is it possible that your sister has hooked a bigger fish?"

Flinching from the sarcasm in his deep voice, Dionis lifted indignant eyes to meet the glitter in his. "There is nothing to be gained by uttering insults, *señor*," she answered quietly, vulnerable to the fact that this was an inn and voices carried on the still night air.

Slowly, he walked to one of the pillars arching the patio and leaning back against it faced her across the top of the brazier. "I am merely trying to get at the truth. When did you first know about it?"

"I wrote to you immediately I received the letter from Angela saying the engagement was at an end. She said she would be in London when I received it."

"And Antonio?"

"Angela didn't say what he intended to do."

"So, she leaves you to face the music. What about the Villa Acacia?"

"My work there is more or less finished. Another week, perhaps, will see it at an end. It was too late to postpone operations. I thought it best to carry on and complete the job."

His face hardened against her as if carved in a mask. "After which you will be joining your sister in London — you the richer for a fat cheque, she having enjoyed a free holiday in Bermuda. Nice going!"

His words struck her like a blow. Dionis stared at him dumbly, her mouth shocked into quivering emotion. And so she stood for shocked seconds, his contempt shaking her to her roots. Then, achieving the right expression for one who had been insulted, her pride outraged, she looked at him with burning indignation. "Nice going, as you say, had we been a couple of adventuresses. As I told you once before, neither Angela nor I are in the least dishonest."

His mouth tilted cynically, cruelly. "You can hardly blame me for drawing my own conclusions."

"I blame you for nothing. I blame myself for taking on a job before I was fully acquainted with the facts. Now I can't wait to get away — but not for the reason you think."

"But you will be joining your sister in London?" he insisted.

"Not necessarily. We've let the flat for six months, and if Angela gets her job back she'll be travelling abroad a great deal."

"Does that mean you will have nowhere to go when you return?" He frowned fiercely.

"No." Dionis, white to the lips, fragile with dark shadows round her eyes, tilted her chin. "I'm not without friends."

"Ah yes. Cesare Delusi," he murmured insinuatingly, and drew a lean hand across a well shaven chin. "And now the financial arrangements concerning Antonio. I understand he is taking care of the cost of the . . ." sarcastically, "improvements to the Villa Acacia? Has he enough in his

157

account to cover them?"

Dionis hesitated, wanting to give Antonio time to settle the account. But this infuriating man already knew of the deficit, most probably. When she answered her voice strangled in her throat. "No, he has not enough to pay the workmen."

"But enough to pay the bills of the materials and..." a distinct pause here, "your fee?"

"My fee doesn't enter into it," she said bitterly. "All I want is for the men to be paid at the end of their contract."

He raised a frankly disbelieving brow. "No? Then why take the job in the first place?"

She stared at him with burning eyes. "I saw it as a chance to further my career," she stated, her voice steady now. Her control had returned, shutting out all pain and weakness. "It was a splendid opportunity, a big thing to be tackled away from home ground. There was no reason why I shouldn't take it. I had already decided to visit the exhibition in Madrid as a kind of holiday between jobs. Maybe the chance to do some constructive work while I was here in a different environment for others to criticize, abuse or even condemn was too great to refuse. However, my work is almost finished." She lifted her small chin defiantly, her face was flushed, her eyes diamond bright with unshed tears. She would have died rather than let him see them. "It's my work, something I adored doing, and I'm proud of it."

Her last words, spoken clearly and distinctly, made the ensuing silence in the dimly lit patio more profound. Then he was striding across in a masterful and determined way, taking few strides to sit down beside her. Resting an arm along the back of the seat, he crossed his legs to support the other arm limply and turned to face her. "You are overlooking one important thing," he said quietly. "The Villa Acacia is my property and I cannot allow any work on it to be done gratis."

"I want nothing." Dionis lowered her eyes, feeling the intentness of his gaze. "All I'm interested in is the workmen, who will expect their pay at the end of next week."

"They will be paid. But I refuse to be in your debt. I shall insist upon you accepting a cheque for your services," he said inexorably.

"It would be kinder if you would forget my part in it," she argued stubbornly, aware of his nearness and finding it suffocating. "The work was done without your approval. Let's leave it at that."

"And if I insist?" Juan asked softly, leaning nearer. When Dionis did not answer he continued in the same low voice, "Since seeing the exhibition in Madrid, have you not the slightest inclination to stay here, say for the summer, and continue with your work?"

"No, definitely not, señor. I intend to leave Spain the moment my work on the Villa Acacia is finished, never to return."

"Does that mean you are taking your sister's word that all Spaniards make unsatisfactory husbands? You appear to believe her implicitly, although she has let you down so ruthlessly. Surely you knew when you came that there was a possibility of her breaking the engagement to Antonio as she had done previous ones?"

"I did. I decided to take the risk. There was always a chance of her having met the right man and settling down."

He said grimly, "Precisely the same idea I had about Antonio. He had never gone so far before in his affairs as to become engaged, which was the reason I questioned the possibility of a reconciliation."

He looked down on the graceful line of her neck, the dejected droop of her head which Dionis shook hopelessly.

"I know Angela. There'll be no reconciliation — you can be sure of that," she stated firmly.

"Pity. Your sister appeared to have a profound influence on Antonio. He needs someone who will make him toe the line. He has no sense of responsibility or any real depth of character. Neither has he any ambition except to do precisely nothing. The only energy he ever exerted was to go through a fortune left to him by his stepfather. He ended up as one of my agents, the worst I have ever had. The rest you know." Juan made a gesture of distaste. "Your sister seems to be the hardened type who could be his saving grace. Incidentally, I am surprised you tolerate her when she behaves so callously to you."

"Angela is my sister, señor. Had Antonio been your brother, no doubt you would have felt the same about him."

"You will be surprised to know that once I treated him like a brother. Tell me, is Signor Delusi married?"

"No."

"You and he seem to be close."

"He is one of my best friends."

"Then I advise you to marry him. I am confident that, as your husband, he would not be long in sorting your sister out. At least you would be free of her." His indrawn breath could have meant exasperation or disgust. Dionis was too miserable to define it. Juan rose to his feet. "*Adios*, Miss Ward," he said slowly, decisively. "You look in need of your bed. My advocate will be getting in touch with you in due course."

enough to leave and return to the inn?

The doctor considered this. "Take my advice, señorita,

CHAPTER XI

THE days passed with Dionis working like one possessed. Work at the Villa Acacia was almost finished when she received two letters from Don Juan's firm of solicitors in Barcelona. One contained a cheque for her services, so fabulous as to take her breath away. The other was to inform her that a man would be calling at the Villa Acacia the following Saturday morning to pay the workmen. With a bitterness she would never have believed herself capable of, Dionis was appalled at the amount of money Juan had seen fit to pay out for something he had not wanted in the first place. She had no intention of accepting his cheque. She would have to decide what to do with it. He was adamant about her being paid. But she was equally adamant about not accepting payment.

On Saturday morning, a poker-faced, bowler-hatted, middle-aged man arrived at the Villa Acacia to pay the workmen. Each man was given a pay packet plus a generous bonus for work promptly done. Later, Dionis entertained the men in the sparkling new kitchen where two bottles of champagne were opened by Paco to celebrate the occasion. Then they all sat down to a generous lunch provided by Señora Lopez which Dionis paid for.

That afternoon Dionis walked through the newly decorated rooms, haunted by Don Juan. Wherever she looked there was some reminder of his generosity – the two lovely floor vases in the lounge, the pretty footstools, the Chinese firescreen and the pedestal with various other items in adjoining rooms. They all seemed to mock at her. For the first time Dionis did not look upon her work with pride. Although she knew it was far and away the best job she had ever attempted it meant nothing to her as she surveyed it with lack-lustre eyes. She felt empty, as if all her zest for living had gone with Juan, who despised her. She would have to write to him thanking him for the cheque and for his generosity to the workmen and herself. After that, nothing. He had gone out of her life, taking with him the enchanted hours colouring her existence, giving her a brief glimpse of a world made beautiful by his presence. There was nothing left for her but to go back to the world she knew without him. Her time in Spain was running out. There were only one or two minor adjustments to be made to the pretty window drapes for the Villa Acacia. The village seamstress had promised to have them ready by midweek. So Dionis waited patiently, giving the Villa Acacia a wide berth until she went to put the final touches to the décor.

She wrote a short letter to Juan thanking him for the generous cheque and for paying the workmen. That done, she had the feeling to be alone, to walk and walk until she was too tired to think. But even that was denied her, for the weather broke overnight and the next two days brought heavy showers of rain and thunder. On Tuesday an invitation to a farewell tea for Nurse Ford at Lemon Tree Cottage came as a lifeline. When Dionis set out to catch the bus at five o'clock, it was still raining. Clad in a white mackintosh with small matching rain hat, she caught the bus armed with a present for Nurse Ford, a soft leather case containing a small manicure set. Pilar was there, her dark eyes shining with a serene happiness. Both mother and child were looking well and Nurse Ford was smiling as if it was all her doing.

The visit did much in sending Dionis's spirits higher than they had been for days. When Doctor Horatio called after his evening surgery to take Pilar and Dionis home the rain had stopped. The red-gold curtain of sky revealed as the clouds passed on sent forth a radiance of light which gave an incredible opulence to the brilliance of the blooms in the garden. The air was like wine. Dionis alone appeared conscious of the radiance of the evening, for the doctor and his fiancée were lost in each other. She occupied the back seat of the car while they sat together in front, and her happiness for them became tinged with loneliness.

Dionis saw the big car seconds after the doctor had left her at the inn. Her heart lurched painfully at the sight of it and her breath caught in her throat. Taking a firm hold of herself, she walked quietly across the deserted courtyard to go upstairs to her room. Don Juan and Señora Lopez were on the landing barring the way to her room. They were looking up at water seeping through a damp patch in the ceiling.

Don Juan was saying, "I would say a tile is at fault on the roof. The workmen could have dislodged it unconsciously when they were building the extensions at the back of the inn. You are sure none of the other ceilings in the house are affected, Señora Lopez?"

"*Si, señor*. I have examined them all except those in Miss Ward's rooms. Ah, here she is now."

Señora Lopez turned to smile warmly at Dionis. Juan's cool smile of greeting was accompanied by a slight inclination of the dark head. Dionis forced a smile. The last thing she wanted was for Juan to go into her bedroom — but it seemed she had no choice.

"We had better take a look," he said, standing aside to allow Dionis to lead the way.

Dionis opened her door and they filed inside. With every nerve on edge, she watched him stride to the windows and open the shutters before he ran a practised eye over the ceiling. He repeated the procedure in the bathroom.

"These are quite in order," he stated, returning to the bedroom with his keen gaze resting briefly on the two suitcases Dionis had packed prior to her departure.

There was a short silence while Dionis stood rigidly with her back against the dressing table. His posy of forget-me-nots was behind her and he must not see them. Dionis had left the little potted flowers out of her case until the day she left.

"Then only the landing ceiling is affected, *señor*." Señora Lopez looked decidedly relieved. "It was fortunate that you happened to call minutes after I saw it."

"I will have it attended to right away," Juan promised smoothly. "I am happy to find the extension standing up to the rain. No leakages there. They were a good team of workmen." He had been smiling pleasantly at the *señora*, but the look he passed to Dionis was slightly cooler. "You were satisfied with the workmen I sent, Miss Ward? No complaints?"

"None, *señor*. I sent a letter to you addressed to the Villa Jacaranda."

"A letter?" The dark eyes looked wary. "Does that mean you have finished at the Villa Acacia? I understood you would be there some time after the workmen had left applying the finishing touches so dear to a woman's heart."

Again Dionis was aware of a slight malice in his deep tones – or was she becoming hyper-sensitive through her love for him? She was beginning to steam in the mackintosh and wished he would go.

"There are one or two small tasks I have to do before I finally hand in the keys," she vouchsafed. "Am I to give them to Paco, *señor*?"

He answered offhandedly in the manner of a man whose mind was occupied elsewhere. "That would be in order, since he will be left in charge. You are not inviting me to see it before you leave?"

Aware of Señora Lopez's interested gaze, Dionis regarded him soberly.

"Surely you don't require an invitation from me to look over your own property?"

"Put like that it does sound absurd, but I had no wish to intrude. I knew I could rely on the workmen I sent. You are perfectly satisfied with the result, Miss Ward?"

In spite of the heat of her body beneath the mackintosh, Dionis quelled a shiver. Remembering his opinion of Angela and herself, she could only assume he was hinting at the cheque he had given to her. Had Señora Lopez not been present, she would have flung it in his face.

"I work with the intention of satisfying my clients. You are quite at liberty to go to the Villa Acacia at any time to

164

see the décor before I leave. I shall be there tomorrow morning. It will be more satisfactory for you to see it in the daylight."

"I will be there at ten-thirty tomorrow," he answered. "Until then, *adios*, Miss Ward."

He walked out of the room with Señora Lopez, one hand thrust negligently into his pocket. Going down the stairs, Dionis heard him talking about putting the inn into a guide book soon to be issued for the benefit of tourists. He had forgotten her already. She stood there with her back against the dressing table, her small face tight with an inward pain of unhappiness. Tomorrow morning the seamstress had promised to deliver the drapes. Thank goodness, she would not be alone with him if she could help it. It would be quite easy to keep the woman there until he had left the Villa Acacia.

There was still the problem of what to do with the cheque. Dionis was no nearer a solution as to what to do with it when she set off for the Villa Acacia after breakfast to see Juan. He would undoubtedly arrive on time and she kept her fingers crossed hoping the seamstress from the village would arrive before him. She was in the kitchen when she heard the voice coming from the open front door.

"*Señorita*, may I come in?"

And there she stood clasping the parcel of furnishings to her ample bosom. Señora Direnso was still pretty, despite her small plump matronly figure. She appeared to be in her forties, with a peach-bloom complexion and abundant blue-black hair.

"By all means," Dionis welcomed her, all smiles. "I am so glad you are here. Don Juan will arrive at any moment to look over the villa."

Relieving Dionis of her parcel, Señora Direnso was quite unprepared for her reaction to her words. Her black eyes widened in dismay.

"Santa Maria!" she breathed. "Don Juan is coming here? Then I must go and return later when he has gone."

"But he is only a man, Señora Direnso. Surely you would

165

not leave me on my own with him? He will not be here long, merely to look over the decorations."

Dionis had spoken quietly, cajolingly. There was a pause while the *señora* digested this. Then she hazarded, "I could stay providing you do all the talking, *señorita.*" The dark eyes were reflective. "I know nothing about your furnishings, so while you are with Don Juan I will attend to my work."

But Dionis doubted whether Señora Direnso would be capable of any work while Don Juan was in the villa. Already her eyes were alight with excitement as she smoothed her already immaculate hair, then drew her hands down her dress in rapid nervous gestures. She had spoken in Spanish and Dionis read the meaning of her words more in her reactions than her actual speech.

The long silver car drew up to the open door of the villa precisely at ten-thirty. Señora Direnso was with Dionis in the hall when he arrived. The *señora* watched his arrival with awe. Ah, here is someone worth waiting for, her expression said.

Aloud, she breathed, "What other *hombre* has the poise the grace of Don Juan – a real *hidalgo*!"

Obviously against him Señorita Direnso was a mere adjunct. But Dionis was not any more composed than her companion. As he slid from the car and walked to the entrance with his light firm footstep, Dionis knew she would always have the memory of sunlight on black well-kept hair, of eyes dark and intense, of a deep alien voice which played on her heart-strings and a superb carriage of arrogance and grace befitting – as Señora Direnso said – an *hidalgo*. She was aware of his width of shoulder in the lightweight suit of pale grey as he filled the doorway.

"*Buenos dias*, Miss Ward, Señora Direnso," he greeted them, in no whit put out at the presence of the seamstress.

"*Buenos dias*," they answered, with Señora Direnso giving a little nervous bob of a curtsy.

He looked momentarily at the *señorita*, then at Dionis, demure and slender in the subdued light of the hall, her fair skin and pretty dress in strong contrast to the dark looks and attire of her companion.

"I trust I am not interrupting anything?" he remarked politely.

"You were expected, señor. Shall we begin upstairs?" Her voice was steady and when Señora Direnso drifted to one of the downstairs rooms, Dionis waited while Juan looked around the hall. He was studying the gold-framed wall mirror set above the lovely inlaid chest he had loaned her. In one corner of the hall was the pedestal topped by an ornate spiralled brass lamp. He made no comment and they walked across the hall where a Spanish rug revealed part of the lovely tiled floor. Dionis went upstairs with him feeling a little odd. Would he approve of her work or disapprove? She clenched her hands. He had to like it. His approval would be balm for her sore heart. She needed it to help her to pick up the threads again when she returned home. But he had such strong beliefs in his own traditions and was such a stickler for detail that her heart began to waver. She would have given much for the cheerful presence of Cesare Delusi in that moment.

In silence, they entered the main bedroom, clean cut and uncluttered with whitewood furniture lining two walls on a sea of blue carpet. Transparent window drapes gathered closely in folds fell regally from ceiling to carpet. Slowly, Juan walked around, hands behind him or reaching out to open cupboards and shallow draws. And Dionis stood meekly by, nothing like as cool as she appeared to be.

Suddenly, he was smiling as if his humour was completely restored by what he had seen. "A restful and delightful room," he commented, adding sincerely, "With a simplicity cleverly contrived by the use of textural rather than colour contrasts. I like it."

Her heart moved, then settled as she spoke her thoughts. "I'm pleased that it meets with your approval. I trust the rest of the décor does too."

He looked down at her with a veiled expression. One dark eyebrow raised as if he would read her inmost thoughts. "You sound doubtful as to my approval of your work, Miss Ward. I have noticed an absence of that spontaneous enthusiasm you have displayed when discussing what you had planned to do."

Dionis replied valiantly, "There's always a feeling of anti-climax when a job is finished, *señor*. One does one's best, but it's too much to hope for all one's efforts to be wholly approved."

"Then take heart, Miss Ward. I could be the exception to the rule."

He continued to view each room with a keenness which missed nothing. The modern kitchen, country style, with its delightful blue and grey Spanish tiles and wipe-clean surfaces met with his full approval, as did the smart lounge. Here deep mauve sofas and chairs looked dramatic against white walls and mauve-shaded lamps on gold-framed, glass-topped tables echoed the richness of overhanging gilt lamps.

Dionis looked at the dark head outlined against the white wall and felt a foolish lump in her throat. "Should you favour another colour scheme, furniture, rugs and lamp-shades can easily be changed," she said rather quickly.

"To me," he replied with complete frankness, "everything appears to have been designed so that the English children and dogs can run around unrestricted with little threat to the furnishings. Is that not so?"

His smile was almost her undoing. It threatened the wall of reserve between them enabling her to answer his few questions with a deferential air. In spite of herself, Dionis warmed to his mood. At the same time she was aware of standing precariously on shifting sand.

"You catch on quickly, *señor*," she said demurely.

"The same can be said of you, Miss Ward, where interior decorating is concerned. Allow me to congratulate you on your work. I wholeheartedly approve of it."

But Dionis could not immediately take it in. She had never known herself so vulnerable to a man's presence, much less his praise of her work. The short cry of pain coming from the kitchen quarters proved someone else's undoing, but not her own. Juan was the first on the scene, with Dionis following. Señora Direnso was sitting on the floor of the kitchen, one leg tucked under her, looking very distressed.

"I slipped," she gasped. "It is my ankle, I think."

Juan picked her up gently to seat her in a chair. Then, kneeling down beside her, he gently explored the region of her ankle with his lean fingers. His expression was thoughtful and he straightened at last to look down sternly on the *señora*.

"There is nothing wrong with your ankle, *señora*. It is not in the least swelled or hurt. You did not slip — you collapsed from fatigue. When did you last eat?"

Señora Direnso was agitated. "I . . . I cannot remember, *señor*. Yesterday some time. But I slipped, I did not collapse."

Juan continued to look at her sternly. "It is no use lying, *señora*. I know. Do you not think it is time you did a little less sitting up all night sewing and allowed that lazy husband of yours to do a little more work?" He put up a hand as she opened her mouth to speak. "You are aware of his duplicity. He no more has arthritis in his back than I have. I am going to take you home and I shall insist that after a meal you go to bed."

Señora Direnso was horrified. "I cannot do that, *señor*. I have work to do and a meal to prepare for my husband and the *niños*."

"You will have no choice, *señora*. I shall send for the doctor if you do not do as I suggest. I shall have a serious talk with your husband and you will find yourself and the *niños* being looked after by a man who must be made to take on his responsibilities."

Helplessly, Señora Direnso looked from his set face to Dionis, who saw the lines of fatigue, the tired shadows beneath her eyes.

Dionis said gently, "You look exhausted, *señora*. I am sure it will be for the best to do what the *señor* suggests. You are clever with your fingers and could easily support the *niños* and yourself without the added burden of a lazy husband. Why not hint to him that you could easily be independent of him if you chose? He would respect you all the more for it and probably pull his weight, making your life much easier. He would also gain the respect of his *niños*."

Juan, tongue in cheek, did not wait for further argument. Tossing Dionis a mocking glance, he scooped up Señora Direnso into his arms and strode out with her. For several minutes after he had gone, Dionis debated whether to attend to the last of her jobs or call it a day. It had certainly been a wearing one up to now. She fingered the parcel Señora Direnso had brought lying on the kitchen table. Poor Señora Direnso! It was terrible to have a lazy husband, especially where the children were concerned. Suddenly, she turned a startled face at the sound of firm footsteps to see Juan in the kitchen doorway.

He was still unsmiling. "Has Señora Direnso finished the work you gave her?" he asked abruptly.

"Yes. This parcel you see here is the last."

He flicked a glance at the parcel on the table. *"Bien,"* he said. "I shall see she receives a cheque for her services."

Dionis kept her eyes lowered on the parcel. It was not the slightest use telling him that she had intended to pay Señora Direnso herself out of her own pocket. Uneasily, she sensed rather than saw his change of mood, as he leaned nonchalantly against the door-frame. She did lift her eyes then, but only in an attempt to catch a glimpse of Señora Direnso waiting in his car. Her action could not have told him more plainly that she wanted him to go. "Do not worry about the *señora*. She is taking a tot of brandy. These jobs you have to do – are they only minor ones?"

"Yes."

"Taking you how long?"

"A few hours." Avoiding his gaze, Dionis saw the dark eyes narrow calculatingly.

"I trust you are not leaving directly your work here on the villa is finished? I did notice you had packed your cases."

"Why not?" she answered stiffly, wondering if that was all he had noticed in her room at the inn. "There's nothing to keep me here."

"Except the natural desire to see a little more of the country before you leave. There is the monastery at Poblet I told you about, and lots of other places which would delight you. You could stay as my guest at the Villa Jacaranda. It would give me great pleasure to show you around."

And prolong her agony as she counted the bitter-sweet days spent in his company? No, thank you. Dionis spoke with a finality which rocked her heart.

"I'm sorry, *señor*, what you suggest is impossible. I have to return to London as soon as I can. I have commitments there which I can ignore no longer. I appreciate your kindness." She fumbled in her bag, unable to meet his eyes, and drew forth a small package. "I forgot this present I have for Señora Direnso. It is a special pair of scissors I sent for. Fortunately they arrived today." Her laugh was fleeting. "Just in time. Excuse me."

He moved aside to allow her through the doorway. She had given the *señora* her present, kissed her cheek in farewell and straightened to find Juan standing in the porch of the villa watching them. Dionis wavered. How did one look on the beloved for the last time without betraying the heartbreak? Of all the ordeals she had had to face this was the hardest of them all.

But she managed it, with anguish rising inside her threatening to choke her words. She never did remember taking the few steps to where he still stood.

"Well, good-bye, *señor*. Thank you for all you have done, and forgive me for all the trouble I have caused." The tears were ominously near, but she forced them back. "I shall give the keys of the villa to Paco tomorrow. Good-bye."

She was conscious of him straightening as she held out her hand. But he did not take it. Instead he gave a stiff formal bow. "Good-bye, Miss Ward. A pleasant journey home."

Her hand dropped simultaneously with her heart.

He strode to the car, slid in behind the wheel and set it in motion. As it slid away, Dionis lifted her hand to Señora Direnso, but Juan kept his eyes front to present his arrogant profile. Well, that was that. Dionis turned slowly back to the villa to hear the scuff of espadrilles on the garden path. Thank heaven for Paco.

"*Buenos dias, Paco*," she greeted him. "Would you come and help me with the drapes, *por favor*?"

When she left the villa Acacia at two to go to lunch, Dionis had finished the last of her jobs. For some reason she could not explain, she had not given Paco the keys. There was no hurry — she had not booked her flight yet. But that was no problem. It was quite possible that she would be able to get a cancelled single seat in any case. What she had to settle, and soon, was the problem of Juan's cheque. She was no nearer a solution when she entered the courtyard of the inn. And there she stood, doubting the evidence of her own eyes.

Someone was sitting at the small table beneath the lemon trees which she usually occupied, someone wearing a smart cream suit, green spotted silk shirt and brown and white buckskin shoes. The sun slanting through the lemon trees played on the dark curly hair and the signet ring on his little finger gleamed as he lifted a drink to his lips.

"Cesare!" she cried delightedly. She ran across the courtyard, bent down before he could rise and kissed him on both cheeks. "When did you arrive?"

He drew back his immaculate cuff and said teasingly, "Exactly twenty minutes and a half ago. Take a seat. Your drink is getting warm." He reached over to drop another chunk of ice from a jug into her glass. "How is business?"

Dionis did not know whether to laugh or cry. She laughed. "I finished at the Villa Acacia this morning. I have the keys still, though." She raised her glass, bordering on the hysterical. "Here's to my next job in dear old London. Cheers!"

"Cheers," he answered, drinking too. Then slowly he lowered his glass to look at her oddly. "Everything all

172

right? You said that with a kind of desperation. Is everything all right?" he repeated.

Cesare Delusi's motive in calling to see Dionis before he returned to London had been prompted by a feeling of concern. He had been more than a little perturbed to see the change in her when he had arrived in Spain. Granted, she had only just recovered from an illness when he saw her at the Villa Jacaranda. Her sparkle had not returned. He had stayed to help her at the Villa Acacia with the hope that he would see it before he left for Italy. But her face was still smaller and paler than he remembered, her eyes curiously shadowed. Take just now as she had entered the courtyard. Before she had seen him there had been none of her youthful spring in her walk. Her expression had become much too serious for a girl who had always lived on the brink of an enchanting smile. He watched her take down part of the cool drink thirstily, saw her make a visible effort to pull herself together.

"Just one problem which I hope you can help me with before I go." She put down her glass and with a hint of the old sparkle put her chin on her hands, elbows on the table. "Tell me about your visit home. Did you enjoy it? How are Momma and Poppa and all the family? Very proud of you, I know."

Cesare's news lasted until Señora Lopez brought the lunch. As they ate Dionis asked him with her usual directness what he was doing in that part of Spain.

"Let's say I'm taking a roundabout route to London in order to see the Villa Acacia. Although you don't know it, you could have started something here which will help our overseas trade."

"I wouldn't want to do any more work here, Cesare," she said quietly. "If that's what you mean."

He raised a brow. "Why not? Did you not enjoy it?"

"In a way. How long will you be staying?"

"One day, two days – it depends."

Dionis had shed a little of her tired look. The lunch was reviving her and she had eaten more than she realized with talking to Cesare. "Then you can see the Villa Acacia before you leave and we might even travel back together." She paused, then plunged. "I'd be grateful if we could go somewhere where we can talk after lunch, if it's all right with you."

"That's easy. I can ring up the local garage to hire a car. We can spend the siesta going for a run in the country or even a dip in the briny. What do you say to that?"

"Lovely," she answered.

The hired car arrived soon after lunch. It was a well sprung and sweetly intimate two-seater.

"Thank goodness the controls aren't cross-eyed," Cesare quipped as he set the car confidently in motion.

Dionis leaned back in her seat listening to the rhythm of the car engine and the gentle swish of the wind as they travelled at speed. Inevitably she thought of Juan and all the ecstasy and delight being with him had brought. It was a depth of emotion she would never experience again with any man. Cesare, one of the best friends she had ever had, with all his masculine charm could never affect her senses with the same swooning bliss. Gradually, Dionis relaxed into a confidential mood. She told Cesare of Angela's broken engagement, her return to London, her fiancé's overdraft and Juan's generosity. When she reached the most difficult part, the payment of the cheque, words failed her. She simply drew the piece of paper from her handbag and put it under his nose.

He gave a low whistle at the amount. "Congratulations! Don Juan must be satisfied with the result. He is not the kind of man to pay out money he did not feel was due."

"But I don't want it, Cesare," she cried. "Nothing would make me accept it!" She bit hard on her lip. It was difficult to convince Cesare of her determination not to accept it. She had not told him of Juan's scathing words about Angela nor his obvious bad opinion of both her and her sister. He would not have hesitated to go to see him and put him right and she did not want someone else to clear her name for Juan's benefit. "I feel awfully guilty about the whole thing. Please help me in getting rid of it."

Cesare swung the car off the main road as he slowed down and stopped the engine as they slid into a side road. Then turning to face her he looked down at her eyes, large and dark in her small face.

"You wouldn't like to sleep on it again? After all, you have earned it," he said evenly.

She shook her head.

"Have you anything in mind? Do you want to get rid of it in one grand gesture for Don Juan to hear about or do you want to get rid of it more discreetly?"

"It's immaterial whether Don Juan hears about it or not. I just don't want it," she insisted. "And he wouldn't accept it back."

"Getting rid of money is much easier than earning it, so it's no problem. Why not wait until you return to London and get rid of it then to some charity or other?"

Again she shook her head. "You might think I'm being sentimental, but I feel the money should remain here in this country. There's so much poverty about in the rural areas. Another thing that bothers me is that I used the money Angela's ex-fiancé had in the bank to pay for the materials for the Villa Acacia, money which he could be needing desperately at this very moment."

"I shouldn't worry about that," Cesare said practically. "Ten to one the man owes rent on the villa."

"If he paid rent. It might have been part of his job as an agent of Don Juan's. Besides, Angela did treat him badly, persuading him to have the villa modernized and then throwing him over."

Cesare mulled this over. "I wouldn't concern myself any more with the affairs of Antonio. Forget him. You might have him seeking you out if you were foolish enough to give him the cheque," he counselled wisely.

"I suppose you're right," she said, feeling rather guilty at the frown between his eyes. Poor Cesare. After all, he was on holiday and did not want to be burdened with her problems. Perhaps she was thinking too hard about it.

Something would come. Meanwhile she could take him over the Villa Acacia in the morning, which was what he had really come for, and help him to enjoy his short visit.

CHAPTER XII

DIONIS had said good-night to Cesare at the end of a very enjoyable evening. They had dined at a restaurant a good car's run from the inn. The meal had been excellent, so had the floor show. A Spanish couple, the woman in a tight-fitting black, flounced dress over a scarlet underskirt, had appeared dramatically with a sinuous grace. Her great dark eyes had flashed as she had clapped her hands above her head and stamped tiny feet to the click of castanets. Her partner, a handsome, virile young man in a tight-fitting black suit and midi-jacket, flaunted all the qualities and vibrant fiery powers of a first-class artist. The fandango they danced carried Dionis along with it. Entranced, she saw a performance of grace, passion and rhythm which left her breathless and slightly dazed at the end of it.

The memory of it lingered when, later, they made their way back to the inn swiftly through the night. There had been an aura of unreality about the whole day, so much had happened. It was a day Dionis would never forget. The evening had been an anti-climax. Cesare had enjoyed it, for he had been smiling, the smile of a man who had earned his leisure at the end of a long hard road leading eventually to success. In the lamplit sanctuary of her bedroom, Dionis envied him his serene contentment. Soon she would be back working, but to her the fruits of success would not be the same. There would be no one to share them with.

Angela would be making her own life, and their grandparents in Canada were well provided for by a wealthy son. Dionis undressed thinking of these things, knowing that being with Cesare this evening had shown only too clearly how desolate she would be without Juan. The wide shoulders of the male dancer had become Juan's after the first few steps, the handsome arrogant profile of the dancer had suddenly been that of the man she would always love.

She slid into pyjamas, appalled at the task ahead of trying to forget him. Could she do it?

Lying in bed, Dionis tried to relax, wishing she could free herself from some inner sense of conflict. Sometimes she felt that a sense of peace and contentment would never be hers again. It had all begun with Juan. How happy and contented she had been on her first night in Spain, how thrilled to talk to Don Fernando and reminisce about her father. She would think of Don Fernando always in the same place, in the lamplit patio of the inn enjoying his cigar and wine and his little gossip with any alien who happened to be there. But in spite of her reasoning and cool common sense, nothing could prevent Juan from entering her thoughts and she fell asleep thinking about him.

After breakfast, the next day, Dionis went along to the Villa Acacia with Cesare and he looked around with a critical eye, much as Juan had done.

"I could not have done better myself," was his verdict at the end of it. "A villa in sunny Spain as lovely as this is worth considering. What do you say?"

He slanted a quizzical brow, growing wary at the deepening of the shadows in her eyes. They had walked outside and were standing in the porch. The garden was really something now Paco had cleaned it up. Dionis found her eyes being drawn to the marble seat she had cleared of weeds the day Juan had arrived. The garden of Eden could not have been lovelier — but it was not for her. Her fingers closed over the keys in her hand in readiness to hand them over to Paco. Then she realized that Cesare was waiting for an answer.

"What about a villa in Italy?" she said, evading the issue. "I believe it is just as lovely." The scuff of Paco's espadrilles on the garden path filled her with relief. The last thing she wanted was for Cesare to know the reason for her reluctance ever to live in Spain. *"Buenos días, Paco,"* she said warmly. "Here are the keys to the villa. I told Don Juan I would give them to you."

His melancholy look was more marked than ever. "So

you will be returning to Inglaterra, *señorita*. I have enjoyed working with you. You are so *simpatica*, so *bonita*. I shall miss you."

"I shall miss you too, Paco." Dionis kissed the leathery cheek, put the keys in his hand and squeezed it. "*Adios*, Paco. God bless."

"You appeared to have made quite a hit with Paco," Cesare remarked dryly as he swung the car on the main road away from the villa. "Where do we go from here?"

"If it's all the same with you, I'd like to call and see how Señora Direnso is. There's a market garden on the way to the village where I can buy some flowers for her." Dionis went on to tell Cesare all about the little seamstress and her collapse at the Villa Acacia. She bought flowers at the market garden and discovered that the owner was an Englishman who had settled in Spain. It was indeed a small world, she thought, as they drove on towards the village.

Señora Direnso lived in one of four cottages situated on the last turn in the road before one entered the village. The rough walls of the small dwelling were whitewashed and a long low wall was slung in front. Dionis could imagine the lazy Señor Direnso sitting on it snoozing the hours away. He was not in sight when they drew up outside. Around the arched doorway vines rioted badly in need of pruning and the garden, where jasmine and plumbago abounded, bore the same air of neglect. Through the open doorway, Dionis could see the stone stairs leading to the upper regions as she knocked and waited.

Cesare had stayed in the car and was the centre of attraction when three small children came from inside the cottage to see who the caller might be. They were clean and neatly dressed. Dionis was wondering how many more little Dirensos there were when a man of medium height, broad of shoulder, came to the door wiping his hands on a white towel. His rather morose expression grew curious at the sight of a slim young English woman on his doorstep.

"*Buenos dias*, Señor Direnso." Dionis spoke in slow halting Spanish. "I have called to ask after Señora Direnso.

How is she?"

"*Por favor*, come in, Señorita . . ."

He paused significantly.

"Ward. My name is Dionis Ward. Señora Direnso has been doing some work for me," Dionis said.

He led her into a room which was clean and comfortable, and gestured her to one of the strong, string-seated chairs placed along the walls. There was a beautifully polished brass lamp on a low Spanish table and a colourful coconut mat on the stone floor. Across the chimney breast a shelf containing earthenware pots and pans caught Dionis's eyes, and a high-backed wooden seat lining the inglenooks each side of the fireplace was gay with bright cushions. A simple dwelling showing withal the pride of peasants who could be as dignified as those in better circumstances, she thought appraisingly.

She sat on the edge of one of the seats, refused a glass of wine and looked up expectantly at Señor Direnso. His wife was in bed under sedation, he said. The doctor had said she was to stay there for a week. She was suffering from exhaustion. And the *niños*? Dionis asked. Who would look after them? Señor Direnso lifted broad lazy shoulders. Don Juan was sending them to the sea that very day for a fortnight while he, Señor Direnso, looked after his wife.

His Spanish was correct and Dionis was able to follow him. He had been quite a handsome man in his youth, she decided, with his classic nose and fine dark eyes. She did not care for his sensuous mouth nor for the bulk of superfluous flesh which made him appear course of fibre. The man definitely needed shaking up, and Don Juan was the man to do it if anyone could. She had a little go in that direction herself. Did the *señor* not think he was a lucky *hombre* that his wife only required a week to recover providing she did not overwork herself again? It might have been more serious. She might easily have died, leaving him with all the *niños* to care for himself. He agreed, and Dionis could see the affair had shaken him up. She stood up, hoping the shaking up would be permanent, gave him the flowers with a message for Señor Direnso that she hoped she would soon be well again, and walked with him to the door. The children were nowhere to be seen. Apparently Cesare had given them pesetas to spend at the village shop.

"Where now?" Cesare asked as they sped along the road back to the inn. "Next stop London?"

"Yes," she answered. One little word that would take her away from Juan for ever. The morning sky was as luminous as a pearl with every tree and shrub, each waving head of golden maize in the fields standing out startlingly clear-cut in the brilliance of light. How she would miss the purity of the air, the wonderful leisurely evenings on the patio, the magic of Juan's presence, his light firm step, his deep voice turning her very bones to marrow. While the urge to leave to escape further hurt was predominant, Dionis dreaded a future which now seemed obscure and hopelessly barren. Her mind and spirit bruised beyond endurance, she listened while Cesare talked of filling in their time should they prove to be unlucky in procuring an air passage right away.

He rang through to Barcelona directly they returned to the inn. There were no seats on any outgoing flight for the next two days, but he would be informed directly there were any cancellations before then. That evening they dined with Don Fernando and his wife. Dionis had packed practically everything in readiness for her departure, including her evening dresses. So for this evening, she had put on a light woollen dress, formal but sweet. Cesare, also wearing a conventional dark suit, was very quiet but observant as he drove through the lovely evening air to Don Fernando's home.

"I like your Don Fernando," he said, paused, then added deliberately, "I like your Don Juan also."

He took a blind corner carefully and missed her startled glance in his direction. Nevertheless, Dionis felt he knew he had jolted her.

"Why do you say that, Cesare?" she cried, trying to make light of it and failing utterly.

"Because you are obviously unhappy over something, and after doing a lot of thinking, I can only assume you are in love. If it isn't Don Juan, then it could be me."

"Oh, Cesare, you dear! I love you, but not in that way," she exclaimed, touched by his concern.

"I didn't think you did — love me, I mean. In any case, I'd only be second best. I lost the only woman I shall ever love. She married a man years older than herself with money." His laugh was bitter. "She couldn't wait for me to leave home and make good. She's sorry now, though."

"You mean she wants you back now you're wealthy?" Dionis asked curiously.

"She doesn't know that. By sheer coincidence she had the next seat to me on the plane when I went home the other week. She was flying to Rome. I told her what I wanted her to know, that I now had a decent job with a good income. She was terribly upset at seeing me, vowed she would love me all her life, but as neither of us believed in divorce that was to be her punishment."

Dionis sighed. "Poor Cesare! You never know — miracles sometimes happen. I hope some day you have your love."

There was not time for further conversation, for they were nearing the Villa Inez where Don Fernando and Doña Inez waited to greet them. There were to be no other guests. Pilar was in Barcelona shopping for accessories for her trousseau while she stayed with friends. Dionis enjoyed the evening more than she had anticipated. It could have been that learning of Cesare's lost love had made her more resigned to her own fate in that direction. It certainly made her more tender towards him. Moreover, Don Fernando was a host with whom it was impossible to be sad, and it helped considerably when Juan's name was not mentioned. It was very late when they left to return to the inn. Don Fernando kissed her hand on parting, begging her to return to Spain soon. Doña Inez seconded his invitation.

Señora Lopez wakened Dionis the next morning to say she had received a long-distance call from Barcelona — two cancellations on the noon plane to London. Ten minutes later Dionis was having breakfast with Cesare. He had carried their cases to the hired car and it was his intention to drive them both to Barcelona airport in it. A garage hand could collect it from there later. Dionis forced herself to swallow a little food in order to stem the numbed, hollow feeling welling inside her before she went upstairs to repair her make-up and collect the rest of her things. Blindly, she looked around a room she would never see again and went quickly downstairs. Señor and Señora Lopez along with Tercia waved them off and they were away. Dionis saw the wild flowers at the side of the road with a painful lurch of the heart. She had forgotten the forget-me-nots.

"Oh, Cesare!" she cried. "I must go back. I've forgotten my little plant."

"Go back?" he echoed with a frown. "Surely they can send it on?"

"But it might die in transit. Please, Cesare," she begged, "it won't take long."

"Is it a special one that you can't get back home to grow from seed?" he wanted to know. "In other words, is it worth going back two miles for?"

"It is to me," she answered firmly. "It's rather a special one."

"So be it," he said good-humouredly, and waited for a wide stretch of road to turn the car round.

Their progress was impeded, as is the case when one is in a hurry – first by a herd of goats who took their time crossing the road picking their way gracefully. The second time it was a farm truck backing out of a field with a load of maize. At last they reached the inn, but were prevented from running to the entrance by a huge delivery van. Dionis slipped from the car, ran past the van to the inn and stopped dead at the sight of the big silver car. Juan! At first the hunger for a glimpse of him overcame every other feeling until common sense came to her rescue. He need not know she was there. The courtyard was empty, but she could hear voices within. Probably the men from the big van parked outside. She went swiftly up the stairs to voices on the landing and once again he was there, looking up at the newly decorated ceiling which had been disfigured days ago by a wet patch.

Señora Lopez was saying, "Thank you for having it attended to, señor. I am sorry you missed Miss Ward. They had only just left when you arrived. I believe Señor Delusi said there would be time for them to have lunch in Barcelona before they caught the plane."

It was too late for Dionis to retreat, for they saw her simultaneously, Señora Lopez with a rather startled look of surprise, Juan with an expression on his face which sent her pulses racing.

"I'm sorry," she said before either of them could speak. "I left something in my room, Señora Lopez. May I get it?"

"By all means, Miss Ward. Señor Don Juan was saying he was sorry to have missed you."

But Dionis had avoided the dark gaze of Juan and had slipped past the señora to her room. The pot of forget-me-nots was in the bathroom. She had taken them in there the previous evening from the dressing table in her bedroom. Picking them up, she looked around wildly for something to wrap them in away from Juan's discerning gaze, but found nothing. It was just possible that he and Señora Lopez had gone downstairs. She listened quietly. There was no sound. Waiting precious minutes, Dionis eventually opened the door stealthily and peeped out. No one there. Walking out of her room, she carried the little pot in triumph; someone moved around the corner of the landing to stand nonchalantly barring her way, and she was staring up at Juan.

"You came for that?" he asked glibly, an eyebrow lifting mockingly at the small pot in her hands. "I don't believe it. You actually came back for these?" He touched the limp flowers with a lean finger. "What did you do – just stick them in the soil?" His eyes narrowed. "You have had them for some time. Is it possible? Can these be the flowers I gave you?" Dionis stood rigid, sensing his nearness along every nerve, his intention to hurt. "Did my giving them to you mean something?"

She had a difficulty in breathing. There was nothing to identify the flowers as the ones he had given to her that day at the Villa Jacaranda. But she could find no feasible answer. The hot colour burned her cheeks as she groped for words. None came.

His fingers gripped her shoulders. "Did it?" he insisted.

Things had gone too far for her to tell him to mind his own business. The next moment she was being propelled backwards gently to her room. With masterful deliberation, the little pot was taken from her and placed on the dressing table, then he was turning her round to face him. Dionis had kept her head lowered. He knew, of course. She could feel his warm breath as he bent his head.

"Tell me why you had to come back for them. Why they were so important?"

He spoke the words with a dangerous softness. Dionis felt the anguish of him knowing the truth of her feelings for him. Pushing him away, she lifted eyes swimming with tears.

"Why do you ask when you already know?" she cried, dashing the tears away childishly with the back of her hand.

"Because I wanted to hear you say it," was the answer as he pulled her roughly into his arms.

Dionis gave a helpless gasp as his mouth crushed her own and his arms tightened around her, crushing the breath from her body. Cesare waiting outside in the car was forgotten as she surrendered to demanding lips and arms that thrilled and terrified her. When at last he let her go, she felt bruised and battered. He was punishing her for the trouble she had caused him – humiliating her in the only way he knew how since he had discovered her feelings for him. It could not be passion darkening the pupils of his eyes into blackness – it was anger. Somehow she contrived to put more space between them.

Bitterly, she said, "You've had your revenge. Now let me go."

She made for the door.

"Are you not forgetting something?" he asked, she thought maliciously.

Blindly, she turned to look at him in all his smiling handsome arrogance, appalled to find she loved him despite his cruelty. Scorn of her own weakness steadied her. She had craved for him as one craves for a powerful drug and, for the time being, his kisses had assuaged that need. When it came again it would be greater than ever. Her voice was as cool as she could make it.

"The flowers? You can keep them."

"No, not the flowers. Me." The last word was spoken against her cheek. He was between her and the door and she was again in his arms. This time he held her gently and murmured something in Spanish between his kisses. When his mouth again claimed her own she felt the passion in him as the pressure of his arms increased. Rough or tender, Dionis found his touch pure delight and she responded ardently to the strength in him. She was as breathless as he was when he released her to draw her down to sit beside him on the bed. Taking her hands in his he openly adored her flushed face and tumbled hair with his eyes. "Did you really think I would let you go?" he whispered.

Dionis looked at him like a bewildered child. "You mean ... you mean ...?"

"I love you, *amada*." He kissed her hands. "You look surprised."

"Surprised?" she echoed with the look of one who wakens from a dream to find it reality. "I had no idea." Her fingers curled around his, wanting to believe that the passion darkening the pupils of his eyes was for her alone.

"Had you not?" Juan raised a tantalizing brow. "Not even when I came all the way from Castellon to look at a damp ceiling at the inn, a job I usually leave to one of my agents? And again when I asked you to be my guest when your work at the Villa Acacia was finished? And this morning when I came post-haste to the inn to find out before you left if you were as shattered as I was at the parting of our ways? Never have I been so ... so angry ... so frustrated, and never so much in love with a woman before!"

"But you advised me to marry Cesare. What if I had taken your advice?"

"Ah, that was not me speaking. It was my anger directed mainly against Antonio and your sister. I tried to convince myself that there was not a pin to choose between the three of you, that you were all out for what you could get. The moment I spoke the words I wanted to recall them. But I am still of the opinion that your sister is mercenary, a calculating piece from whom you are better away." His eyes had hardened as he spoke. Now they twinkled devilishly as he leaned forward to kiss the end of her nose. "Now tell me that you forgive me for doubting you and for saying harsh things about you that were not true."

"I forgive you."

"Because?"

"Because I love you." Dionis smiled through her tears. "I've never loved anyone before as I love you. I think I must have loved you from the start. When Angela mentioned that you were the owner of the Villa Acacia I could not bear the thought that you might be hurt by her desire to strip your villa and furnish it to suit herself." A warm flush covered her creamy skin. "I fell for you in more ways than one at our first meeting in the garden of the Villa Acacia."

Juan gave a loving pinch to her flushed cheek, a laugh in his dark eyes, a tender passionate look of a man who had found his heart's desire.

"I fell in love with you irrevocably the day I gave you the posy of forget-me-nots. You caressed them with an ecstatic cry of joy and suddenly I wanted you to look at me like that, to touch my face, to give me the pleasure of knowing that I, Juan Stebelo, was the only man who could bring you pure joy and ecstasy." He drew her hands up to his face and she caressed it gently.

"I never imagined I would ever be able to do this," she murmured. "Doña Dolores, yes. Never me."

He gripped her wrists. "Why Dolores? There is no bond between us."

So Dolores had lied. But Dionis had it in her heart to pity her.

"You obviously admired her, and her name was linked with yours on occasions."

He shrugged. "My name has been linked with *señoritas* since I was in my teens. I was once betrothed to a younger sister of Dolores, but nothing came of it. I was largely to blame for that — I had no inclination to marry, and certainly not Antonia, who was more like a sweet little sister to me than anything else. She is happily married now, as you and I shall be very, very soon." He leaned forward with the ardent look of a lover. "I give you three weeks to prepare for our wedding, which will take place at Castellon, my family home. In the meantime, you will be one of a number of guests I shall invite to the Villa Jacaranda. Dolores will not be included. She has gone home. As for the Villa Acacia, we shall keep it for a place to stay on occasions. Not too often, for I want my children to grow up in the Spanish way of life. When we return from our long honeymoon, my sister Rosalba will be married."

Dionis was staring aghast. "But three weeks? There's so little time!" Only then did she remember Cesare waiting in the car outside. "Oh, my goodness!" she cried. "I forgot Cesare. We must go to him immediately." She was on her feet and Juan allowed her to pull him up reluctantly. "There was nothing between Cesare and myself. He lost the only woman he will ever love years ago to someone else. It's my belief he'll wait for her forever if need be."

The first thing they saw on reaching the door of the inn were Dionis's cases, placed there by Cesare. There was no sign of him. The big truck standing outside the inn when she had arrived had gone. So had Cesare's car from higher along the road.

Dionis looked at Juan helplessly. "He's gone. Cesare has gone!"

He smiled. "Signor Delusi is a very intelligent man."

"But I don't understand. How did he know about us?"
She looked at him curiously. "Come to that, how did you
know we were leaving this morning? There are other things
which puzzle me too. When you sent the man to pay the
workmen at the Villa Acacia, how did you know the day
they were finishing there? There was that time you sent the
men to start work, again on the right day, and . . . and . . ."
It was quite a feat for Dionis to think rationally when his
burning gaze was as tangible as a kiss. "Oh yes . . . the
cheque you gave me. It was far too generous and you know
it. How could you expect me to accept it? I shall . . ."

But what Dionis had decided to do with the cheque was
never disclosed — at least to Juan, who had closed her mouth
effectively with his own. And as she swooned, crushed
against him, Dionis did not care a jot if Señora Lopez did
come out and see them. She did not care if the whole world
saw them. She was going to marry the man of her heart.
And because she had found him through Angela he must
not be too hard on her sister. In that moment Dionis loved
not only Angela but the whole world, and she loved Juan
most of all.

This month's
Harlequin Romances

Every month eight great new stories in the world's most popular series of romances.

No. 1753	Nan Asquith	No. 1757	Dorothy Cork
TIME MAY CHANGE		THE GIRL AT SALTBUSH FLAT	
No. 1754	Lucy Gillen	No. 1758	Elizabeth Hunter
THE PRETTY WITCH		THE CRESCENT MOON	
No. 1755	Penelope Walsh	No. 1759	Marjorie Lewty
SCHOOL MY HEART		THE REST IS MAGIC	
No. 1756	Kay Thorpe	No. 1760	Katrina Britt
AN APPLE IN EDEN		THE GUARDED GATES	

Still only 60¢ each

Harlequin Presents...
75¢ each

No. 34   Stormy The Way
ANNE HAMPSON

No. 35   Seen By Candlelight
ANNE MATHER

No. 36   Love's Prisoner
VIOLET WINSPEAR

All titles available at your local store. If unable to
obtain titles of your choice, you may order from

HARLEQUIN READER SERVICE
M.P.O. Box 707
Niagara Falls, N.Y. 14302
Canadian address:
Stratford, Ontario, Canada.

Golden Harlequin Library

A Treasury of Harlequin Romances!

Many of the all time favorite Harlequin Romance Novels have not been available, until now, since the original printing. But on this special introductory offer, they are yours in an exquisitely bound, rich gold hardcover with royal blue imprint. Three complete unabridged novels in each volume. And the cost is so very low you'll be amazed!

Handsome, Hardcover Library Editions at Paperback Prices! ONLY $1.95 each volume.

This very special collection of classic Harlequin Romances would be a distinctive addition to your library. And imagine what a delightful gift they'd make for any Harlequin reader!

Start your collection now. See reverse of this page for **SPECIAL INTRODUCTORY OFFER!**

v